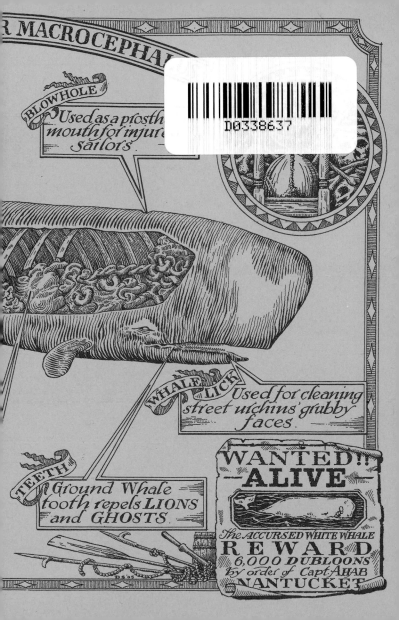

THE PIRATES!

In An Adventure With Whaling

Also by Gideon Defoe

THE PIRATES!
IN AN ADVENTURE WITH SCIENTISTS

THE PIRATES!

In An Adventure With Whaling

Gideon Defoe

Weidenfeld & Nicolson

LONDON

First published in Great Britain in 2005
by Weidenfeld & Nicolson

1 3 5 7 9 10 8 6 4 2

© Gideon Defoe 2005

Map copyright © Dave Senior 2005

A CIP catalogue record for this book is available
from the British Library

ISBN 0 297 84901 8

Printed in Great Britain by
Clays Ltd, St Ives plc

Weidenfeld & Nicolson
An imprint of the Orion Publishing Group
Orion House, 5 Upper St Martin's Lane,
London WC2H 9EA

www.orionbooks.co.uk

To Sophie,

who still has a quarter of a million pounds
of which I have not seen a single penny,
even though this is the
second entire book
that I have dedicated to her.

CONTENTS

One

I BATTLED A TON OF TURTLE!

'That one looks almost exactly like a whale!'
'No it doesn't. It looks like a pile of rags with an ant stood on them. But for some reason the ant only has five legs.'

'It's more like a cutlass. Or a beautiful mermaid lady.'

'It's a big seagull!'

'It's a skull!'

The pirates were busy lying on their backs on the deck of the pirate boat trying to decide what clouds looked like. Most days this enterprise would end up with the pirates having a brawl about whether a cloud would taste more like a marshmallow or a meringue if you could eat one, but today, before the pirates even had the chance to get their cutlasses out or pull angry faces at each other, there was a sudden crack, a shower of dust and splinters, and with a tremendous crash the boat's mast fell down on top of them.

The mast completely flattened the pirate who liked to show off how much he knew about wine, whilst the pirate with a hook for a hand found himself engulfed in a billowing white sail, and he was soon chasing the other pirates about, pretending to be a ghost. There was such a commotion none of the pirates even noticed the galley doors swing open and the Pirate Captain himself step out onto the deck. The Pirate Captain had taken to wearing a dashing maroon smoking jacket and a blousy white shirt that had most of the buttons undone to reveal the glossy hairs on his chest. His chest hairs were almost as well-conditioned as the hairs in his luxuriant beard, which many of the crew felt to be one of the seven wonders of the oceanic world. If the pirate crew had been asked to list the seven wonders of the oceanic world in full they would have confidently said, in ascending order: 1) the Lighthouse at Pharos; 2) the Colossus of Rhodes; 3) Lulworth Cove; 4) those jellyfish that light up; 5) Lobsters; 6) Girls In Bikinis; 7) the Pirate Captain's fantastic beard.

'What in blazes is going on, you oily wretches?!' the Pirate Captain bellowed.

The pirates all dusted themselves down, and the pirate with a hook for a hand sheepishly took off the sail and stopped doing ghost noises.

'Sorry, Captain,' said the pirate in green. 'We were just discussing what the clouds looked like when the mast fell down again.'

The Pirate Captain stepped over the bits of broken mast and tangled rigging and squinted up at the cloud that the pirates were looking at.[1] He clicked his tongue thoughtfully.

'It looks,' he said, after a little deliberation, 'like my stentorian nose with a bottle of grog next to it.'

The pirates all nodded, and slapped their foreheads, because that was *exactly* what the cloud most looked like, and they could all see it now the Pirate Captain had pointed it out.

'Listen, lads. Looking at clouds is all well and good,' said the Captain sternly, 'but some of us have important piratical work to do. So try and keep the noise down. Maybe tie a few knots, or something quiet like that.'

And with a waggle of his eyebrows and a wave of his cutlass, the Pirate Captain swept back through the big oak doors to his office. As the doors slammed shut, one of them fell off its hinges, which slightly diminished the imperious effect he had been going for.

---

1 Clouds that look like things tend to be fair-weather cumulus clouds, which have a lifetime of just 5–40 minutes.

Back in his office the Pirate Captain sat at his desk and tried to get on with some work. As usual he spent a few minutes arranging his quills and paperweights. After that he tapped a pencil against his teeth. Then he tried balancing an inkpot on his nose. Finally he got up and walked around the room a little bit, hoping he might get some inspiration from the various portraits of himself that he had hung up about the place. He'd had some new ones done since their last adventure. There was a black-and-white painting that showed him with his shirt off tenderly cradling a baby. There was one of him emerging from an old boot alongside a giant kitten. And next to that was an actual 'Wanted' poster[2], which had a grainy picture of the Pirate Captain on it, and a bounty of ten thousand doubloons. The Pirate Captain stopped in front of a mirror and practised pulling the same face that he was doing in the Wanted poster, until a tentative knock at the door sent him diving back behind his desk. He scratched his forehead to show how deep in thought he was and said, 'Come in!' in his best working voice. The pirate with a scarf poked his head around the door.

'Hello Number Two,' said the Pirate Captain.

'Hello Pirate Captain,' said the pirate with a scarf, who for some reason was carrying the boat's steering

---

2 In 1718 the Governor of Virginia offered a reward of £100 for the capture of the notorious Blackbeard. That's about £10,769 in nowadays money, so it probably wouldn't have been worth the bother.

wheel. 'I was hoping I could have a word?'

'Of course!' The Pirate Captain waved for him to take a seat. 'Actually, I'm glad you're here – you can help me with this work I'm doing.' He looked at his second-in-command seriously. 'I'm making a list of when it's acceptable for a pirate to cry.'

'That sounds very important, Captain,' said the pirate with a scarf, fiddling anxiously with his eye-patch. He had a delicate topic he wanted to broach, and you never could tell with the Captain if he might not fly into one of his terrible rages, because he prided himself on being unpredictable, like the ocean.

'So far I've got: one – when holding a seagull covered in oil. Two – when singing a shanty that reminds him of orphans. Three – when confronted by the unremitting loneliness of the human condition. Four – chops. I've just written the word "chops". Not really sure where I was going with that one. Any ideas?'

'It's a very good list, Captain,' said the pirate with a scarf, wondering why the last few zeros on the Captain's Wanted poster were in a different colour ink from the others. 'But there's something a few of the other pirates wanted me to ask you about.'

'Oh dear,' said the Pirate Captain, noticing the worried look on the scarf-wearing pirate's otherwise rugged face. 'Nothing relationship-based, I hope? You know how I'm not very good with emotional issues.' The Captain paused and looked out of the porthole. 'I think the problem is I'm just not very interested in them.'

'No, Captain. Nothing like that.'

'Well then. Fire away!'

'It's the boat, Captain. I don't know if you've noticed, and it would be fair enough if you hadn't, what with you being so busy making lists and all, but ... well ...' The scarf-wearing pirate tried to think of the most tactful way to put it. 'She's in a bit of a state.'

The Pirate Captain looked thoughtfully at the fraying wooden beams and the big patches of mould on the ceiling. 'Oh, I think "state" is a bit harsh. "Full of character" is probably the phrase you're after.'

'That's the third time this week the mast has fallen down, Captain.'

'Good thing too. Keeps the lads on their toes!'

'It's not just the mast, Captain,' the scarf-wearing pirate persisted. 'The cannons don't work properly. Several of the pirates have been getting nasty splinters, from the deck being so rotten. There's tar all over the place. And this,' he held up the boat's wheel and waggled it about, 'just came clean off in my hands.'[3]

'Arrrr.' The Pirate Captain stroked his beard. 'I suppose we need that for the ... the uh ...'

'Steering, sir. It moves the rudder.'

'Of course, the rudder. I knew that. The rudder's the one with the portholes, isn't it?'

---

3 The ship's wheel first replaced the tiller in 1705.

'That's the forecastle, Captain.'

'Yes, the forecastle. Anyhow, pass it over here.' The Captain took the wheel, gave his trusty number two a reassuring wink, strode over to the back of his office and hung it on a spare nail that was sticking out from the wall. 'Paint a few numbers round the edge, it's got the makings of a nice dartboard, don't you think? Problem solved.'

Before the Pirate Captain had time to congratulate himself on this clever idea, the steering wheel thudded onto the carpet, taking the nail and a piece of the boat's wall with it. A spray of seawater jetted into the Captain's office and knocked an astrolabe off his mantelpiece. The Pirate Captain frowned.

'Look at that. It's made a little hole,' he said. But without missing a beat he picked up one of his portraits – the one of him smiling standing next to a lady-boy on the beach in Thailand – and propped it up over the leak.

'I don't think you can really just cover up holes with pictures, Captain,' said the pirate with a scarf sadly, as a steady stream of water went on dribbling down onto the carpet.

'Nonsense,' snorted the Pirate Captain, briefly pulling aside another painting to reveal a second nasty-looking gash in the wall. 'See. That's much worse, and it's been there for ages!'

The Pirate Captain grinned, but the pirate with a scarf just gave him a reproachful look.

'The boat's really not safe, Captain. What if there was a storm? She wouldn't hold together for a minute.'

'I suppose a few of the lads might get washed out to sea,' agreed the Captain with a shrug. 'But, like my wise old Aunt Joan always says, it's a harsh life out on the ocean.'

'It's not just the pirates I'm thinking of,' said the scarf-wearing pirate. He paused meaningfully. 'What about your Prize Ham?'

He pointed at the big glass-fronted display case in the corner of the room. Inside the case hung the Pirate Captain's pride and joy – a huge glistening honey-roast ham.[4] It was about as close as you could get to the platonic ideal of a ham, if Plato had spent more time discussing hams and less time mucking about with triangles. It gleamed like a lumpy pink jewel where the sunlight from the porthole caught its honey glaze. There was even a little silk bow tied around the thin end.

'Oh goodness,' said the Pirate Captain, looking lovingly at the ham. 'You're right. I don't think I could bear the thought of anything happening to her. And you know I can't say no when you do those big sad eyes at me.' He slumped back into his chair. 'What were you thinking?'

---

4 The most expensive ham in the world is *pata negra iberico* ham, which costs around £13 per 100 grams. Each pig spends its brief life feasting on 8kg per day of the sweet, oily holm oak acorns found in the Mediterranean woodlands where they are raised.

'We're not far from Nantucket, Captain,' said the pirate with a scarf, pointing at the nautical chart that the Captain had been using as a blotter.

'I know a limerick about Nantucket,' said the Pirate Captain brightly.

'It's where Cutlass Liz has her pirate boatyard,' said the pirate with a scarf, trying his best to keep the conversation on topic, which could be difficult with the Pirate Captain. 'I thought we might stop off and get the boat fixed up properly. Then after that we could have an adventure, maybe with spies or something.'

'Hell's bells,' exclaimed the Pirate Captain. 'Cutlass Liz! The Butcher of Barbados. I don't think they hand out those sort of nicknames for no good reason.'

The pirate with a scarf nodded ruefully. 'It's pretty hard to find reputable boatyards that are prepared to deal with us pirates,' he pointed out.

'Yes, I suppose you're right. Sometimes I wonder if I should have taken up a more respectable line of work. Did I tell you how my mother was hoping I would be an architect?'

'I'm sure you'd have made a brilliant architect, Pirate Captain.'

'I'd have liked building those little models best. With the cut-out people.'

The Pirate Captain drifted off for a moment, thinking about his career choices.

In the boat's dining room the rest of the pirates were already tucking into their lunch. On board a pirate boat it wasn't considered rude to start before everybody was present, and you could even put your elbows on the table. Those were just two of the perks that attracted people to the piratical life. The Pirate Captain strode in followed by the pirate with a scarf to tell the crew the news. He picked up his 'Number One Boss' mug that the pirates had given him for his last birthday and downed it in one gulp. Then he banged the mug on the table.

'Listen up lads – and lady,' said the Pirate Captain with a nod to Jennifer, who had joined them on their last exciting adventure. 'What's the single most important thing in the life of a pirate?'

The crew all looked deep in thought. There were a few whispered discussions. Then the pirate in green put his hand up.

'Is it love?' he asked.

The Pirate Captain rubbed the back of his neck. 'Yes, all right. That's probably true. But after that, what's the next most important thing?'

'Respecting his or her mother?' suggested the pirate with gout.

'Fair enough,' conceded the Pirate Captain. 'You'd be nowhere without your mothers. But then what? What's the third most important thing?'

The crew looked stumped.

'His pirate boat!' roared the Captain. 'It's come to my attention that the old girl's a little past her best. And I can hardly maintain my reputation as a debonair terror of the High Seas with bits falling off the boat all the time, can I? So you'll be pleased to know that we're paying a visit to Cutlass Liz's boatyard.'

The pirates didn't look very pleased at all. Most of them look petrified.

'Cutlass Liz!' exclaimed the sassy pirate.

'They say she's as deadly as she is beautiful!' said the pirate in green.

'I heard she ate twenty babies, just to show her crew how ruthless she was!' said the albino pirate.

'Twenty whole babies all in one sitting!'

'You tried that once, didn't you, Pirate Captain? To terrify that admiral?'

'But there weren't any babies around at the time.'

'I remember that. We drew faces on a load of hams instead. Ham babies!' A few of the pirates laughed as they remembered their adventure with the ham babies. Then they remembered about Cutlass Liz and looked worried again.

'Oh, I'm sure her reputation has been exaggerated,' said the Pirate Captain, helping himself to another mug of grog. 'You know how us pirates get. She's probably just a bit stroppy now and again. And besides – who *hasn't* slit a man's belly open for looking at them cock-eyed?'

Two

SKULL HUNT ON
PYGMY ISLAND!

And so the pirate boat arrived at the island of Nantucket. Sailing past the harbour, it struck the pirates that the whole place seemed slightly one-note.[5] The quayside inns all had names like 'The Blue Whale's Rest' or 'The Narwhal's Arms', and everywhere you looked there were big bronze statues of grimacing whales with harpoons sticking out of their sides and stalls that only seemed to sell 'I Had A *Blubberly Time* In Nantucket' t-shirts and tatty-looking snowstorms with whales in them. They pulled up alongside Cutlass Liz's boatyard, and the Pirate Captain couldn't help but

---

5 In the early nineteenth century Nantucket was the whaling capital of the world. Whaling voyages would set out from port in search of 'greasy luck', which apparently the whalers could say without laughing.

notice how shabby the pirate boat looked parked next to all the shiny new pirate boats that lined the side of the dock. He hoped that the holes in her hull and bits of rigging held together by tape would say 'rustic charm' rather than 'barely afloat'. There was a sign hung on the boatyard gate:

CUTLASS LIZ!
PIRATE BOATS USED & NEW
NO DOGS, ROYAL NAVY OR SENSITIVE TYPES

The pirates looked around, but apart from some seagulls kicking about and a couple of unkempt old men shouting prophetic tales of doom at sea to nobody in particular, the place seemed deserted.

'Looks like she's not about,' said the albino pirate. 'Might as well be going.'

'Yes, we did our best,' said the pirate in green.

'No point dilly-dallying,' said the pirate with gout.

The Pirate Captain was just about to ask if they were pirates or pignuts, when Cutlass Liz made her dramatic entrance. In his time the Pirate Captain had made a number of dramatic entrances of his own – not always intentional it had to be said, as quite often they were the result of him accidentally setting himself on fire – but even he had to admit that Cutlass Liz's dramatic entrance set an extremely high dramatic-entrance standard. A terrified-looking man in a tattered coat came sprinting desperately across the cobblestones. He stopped for a moment, stared wildly about, looked up, and shrieked. The pirates all looked up too, just in time to see Cutlass Liz come sliding down the mainsail of one of the boats, swing across the dock on a piece of rigging, and land with an athletic somersault right in front of the terrified-looking man, who she lifted off his feet by one ear. Cutlass Liz changed the colour of her hair as often as the Pirate Captain ate mixed grills, but at the moment it was a vivid red, which went well with the bloodstains on her blouse. She didn't have a luxuriant beard, but otherwise she cut quite the piratical dash: a huge sapphire necklace that spelt 'LIZ' hung around her neck, and in her belly button she wore a gigantic diamond shaped like a skull, which was rumoured to have been a gift from Napoleon, who she had dated briefly as a teenager. On any other pirate, the necklace and the diamond together might have looked a little bit much, but Cutlass Liz was famed for having the best face in the entire eastern seaboard, and so she somehow carried it off. If he had been meeting her a hundred and fifty years later, the Pirate Captain might have been struck by how much Cutlass Liz looked like the actress Julie Christie from around the time of *Billy Liar* or maybe *Darling*, but he wasn't, so he just thought she looked fantastic. The pirate with a scarf sighed, because he knew how the Pirate Captain tended to get around attractive women.

'I can pay, Cutlass! I can pay! One more day!' pleaded the man with a tattered coat.

'Too late, Jericho Leith,' said Cutlass Liz, grinning from ear to ear. 'Two minutes too late!'

And with that, she took out her cutlass and did some unspeakable things to the unfortunate Jericho Leith. The Pirate Captain stood and watched politely, occasionally wiping a bit of blood from his eyes. Finally, just when he was starting to think that it might go on all day, Jericho Leith let out a horrifying gurgle and slumped down dead. Cutlass Liz deftly kicked his body into the harbour, and turned on her heel to face the pirates.

'You must be Cutlass Liz,' said the Pirate Captain, doffing his hat[6] and doing a little bow. 'I'm the Pirate Captain. You've probably heard of me. Possibly from one of those libellous accounts of my adventures that seem to be doing the rounds. I'm a successful pirate, you know.'

'Is that a fact?' Cutlass Liz arched a perfectly shaped eyebrow, and went on wiping customer innards off her hands with a flannel.

'Oh yes. I lead an extremely glamorous lifestyle,' said the Pirate Captain, hoping she had noticed how many of his best lace ribbons he had tied in his beard that

---

6 The piratical tri-corn hat evolved from the 'cocked hat' worn in the English Civil War, where one side of a wide-brimmed hat was tipped up to allow firing of a musket from the shoulder.

morning. 'And I'm really very well off. Because of all the treasure.'

The pirate with a scarf bit his lip. This wasn't the first time he had heard the Pirate Captain be a bit less than honest about his financial status when talking to a lady.

'I've got more treasure chests than I know what to do with,' continued the Captain. 'All fit to bursting with silvery doubloons and pearls and sapphires and rubies, and those green ones too.'

'Emeralds?'

'Yes, that's it, emeralds. Buckets of emeralds. It's a wonder the boat can even move.'

'Tell me,' said Cutlass Liz, 'what kind of pirate captain doesn't have a crew?'

The Pirate Captain looked about and realised that apart from the pirate with a scarf, his crew were nowhere to be seen.

'Aarrrr. It's just they're all a little bit scared of you,' said the Pirate Captain apologetically. 'Come on, you coves!'

The pirates reluctantly slunk out from behind various barrels and piles of old fish. Several of them held their hands over their faces in the mistaken belief that if they couldn't see Cutlass Liz then she couldn't see them.

'You know I once ate twenty babies?' said Cutlass Liz, looking them up and down. The crew all nodded fearfully.

'I'm sure babies taste a lot better than pirates,' said

the albino pirate. 'Because they'd be fresher. And not as salty.'

Cutlass Liz stared incredulously at the albino pirate. The albino pirate was so frightened that he somehow managed to go even whiter than usual. For a moment nobody said a thing. Then Cutlass Liz threw back her head and let out a laugh that sounded like a delicate foghorn. She pinched one of the albino pirate's cheeks and slapped him hard on the back. 'I like you. I don't know what you are, but I like you. What are you? Some kind of a milk bottle?'

'I don't think so,' said the albino pirate, trembling.

'Well you're all right. I suppose you swabs are here to get your boat fixed up?' said Cutlass Liz, putting her hands on her hips.

'Yes, please. I mean to say, if that would be all right. Not if you're too busy or anything,' said the scarf-wearing pirate.

Cutlass Liz looked at the ramshackle old pirate boat and frowned. 'Is that a piece of *gammon* you've patched up the side with?'

'You'd be surprised how effective a properly cooked bit of gammon can be at keeping out the weather,' explained the Pirate Captain, making sure to touch his hair, because he remembered hearing that touching your own hair was a good way to be flirtatious with someone.

'And she seems to be listing rather badly.'

'Oh, that's just because I like to keep my boats at a jaunty angle. It's to demonstrate that I don't take life too seriously.'

'Not having a mast? Does that demonstrate anything in particular?'

'Ah, no. Not as such.'

'Sorry, boys,' said Cutlass Liz with a shrug. 'I don't think there's much I can do for her. But have you thought about trading her in? I do part exchange, you know.'

'How much do you think the old girl's worth?' asked the pirate in green.

'She's sturdier than she looks,' lied the scarf-wearing pirate.

'Yes. And you're not just getting a boat,' said the sassy pirate. 'I reckon there must be about five hundred pounds of barnacles stuck to her hull. That's got to be worth a bit.'[7]

'And it's full of rats,' added the albino pirate helpfully. He was going to say about the mushrooms that were growing out of the carpet in the galley as well, but the Pirate Captain cut in before he had a chance.

'She's not on fire. That's got to count for something.'

'Well ...,' Cutlass Liz tapped the pirate boat's hull with her boot, and it made a sort of squelching noise.

---

7 The cement exuded by barnacles is an extremely tough protein polymer. It is twice as strong as the epoxy glue used on the space shuttle. Also, the barnacle penis is ten times as long as the rest of its body.

'You're robbing me, but I could probably stretch to fifty doubloons. Might get some useful kindling out of her. What are you looking to replace it with?' She waved at the various types of boat that were sat about her boat-yard. 'I've got pirate sloops, pirate galleons, pirate yachts, pirate schooners, pirate pedalos ... anything take your fancy?'

'I was thinking something to match my fearsome and larger-than-life personality,' said the Pirate Captain. 'I like the look of that big one over there.'

Cutlass Liz nodded approvingly. 'The *Lovely Emma*? She can outrun anything in the Royal Navy, and short of being attacked by a sea monster, that double-layered hull makes her virtually unsinkable. And there's plenty of room for all that treasure of yours.'

The pirates all looked up at the *Lovely Emma*. The pirate with a scarf counted a full thirty gleaming cannons. Some of the less practically minded pirates noticed she had the most striking figurehead they had ever seen – a smiling lady carved out of oak. From the waist up the smiling lady left almost nothing to the imagination, and several of the younger pirates' eyes grew as wide as saucers.

'Yes, that's the kind of thing we're after. How much does she cost? After you've knocked off the fifty doubloons, that is?'

'Six thousand doubloons.'

The Pirate Captain almost dropped his cutlass. He

took a moment to compose himself and pretended to be thinking it over.

'It's a bit flash, is the thing. I don't want people thinking I'm vulgar. How about that one over there?'

'That's the *Perch*. She's only five hundred doubloons,' said Cutlass Liz. 'And she comes with a free ham.'

'Aaarrr. Still a bit on the showy side. What about that one?' said the Pirate Captain, pointing disappointedly to the smallest boat in the lot.

'The *Sea Slug*? Two hundred doubloons.'

Before the Pirate Captain had time to say that maybe he wasn't that bothered about buying a new boat at all, mainly because of unspecified environmental concerns he had about them, he was interrupted by a shout from the other end of the docks.

'If it isn't my old friend the Pirate Captain!' bellowed a familiar voice. The Pirate Captain froze. All the blood drained from his face, though you wouldn't really notice this because of his luxuriant beard. But if beards had blood in them, it would have drained from that as well.

'Black Bellamy!' said the Pirate Captain, thinking that his day couldn't get much worse. Black Bellamy was the roguish rival pirate who the pirates had most recently encountered in their adventure with scientists. He was famous for having a beard that went up to his eyeballs and a matching rakish charm. There were several reasons why the Pirate Captain and Black Bellamy didn't get on, but the main one was that Black Bellamy was the Pirate Captain's evil nemesis, which obviously put quite a strain on the relationship.

'Buying yourself a new boat?' said Black Bellamy, beaming. 'Not before time!'

The Pirate Captain scowled. 'What are you doing here, you cove?'

'You know, whenever we meet you're always calling me a cove or a fiend or something terrible like that. A pirate's feelings could be quite hurt. I'm just picking up a few piratical supplies from Lizzie here. That the one you're getting?' Black Bellamy looked over at the *Sea Slug* and pulled a face. 'She's very nice. Compact. I think the French call it *bijou*. Sometimes I find all the space on the *Barbary Hen* such a burden. So much easier to keep something as small as that tidy.'

'As a matter of fact,' the Pirate Captain said with a sniff, 'I'm buying this one.' And he pointed straight at the *Lovely Emma*. The pirate with a scarf buried his face in his hands.

'Goodness,' said Black Bellamy, obviously impressed. 'The pirating business must be treating you well. I'm surprised there's so much money in, what was it ...? Zoological specimens?'

'Yes, I've been meaning to have a word with you about that.'

'An honest mistake,' said Black Bellamy holding his hands up with a cheeky shrug.

'You won't be disappointed with her, Pirate Captain,' said Cutlass Liz, giving him a playful tug on his beard. 'How do you plan to pay? Doubloons or treasure?'

The Pirate Captain paused. 'Aaarrrr. Thing is, all my treasure is a little tied up at the moment. It might take me a couple of weeks to get my hands on it.'

'Didn't you say it was all in treasure chests? On board your boat?'

'I did. That's to say, it is. But, uh, I have about a hundred treasure chests,' said the Pirate Captain, thinking on his feet, 'and that means about a hundred different keys. Obviously, for security purposes, I don't label either of them. So there's no knowing which key fits which chest.'

The Pirate Captain was quite pleased with this explanation, but Cutlass Liz just frowned.

'It shouldn't take too long to open one chest?'

'You'd think that, wouldn't you?' said the Pirate Captain. 'But – ah – you're working on the assumption that I try the chests in some sort of systematic order. Whereas what I'll actually do is try random keys in random chests, making no real note of which chest or which key I have already tried. It could take days.'

Cutlass Liz gave the Pirate Captain a look. It was the same sort of look as Jennifer sometimes gave him when he said he hadn't realised the boat's shower was occupied.

'You're not a time-waster, are you, Pirate Captain?'

said Cutlass Liz, turning a pretty shade of pink round her décolletage. 'Because I save my most terrible cutlass work for time-wasters. Time-wasters and actors.'

'Can I just say,' said the Captain, deciding to change tack, 'that I've always approved of women at sea. A lot of pirates will tell you that the closest girls should get to nautical matters is making seaweed albums, or those boxes covered in shells. But I don't think that at all.'

Cutlass Liz tapped the blade of her cutlass.

'All right,' said the Pirate Captain with a sigh. 'I wasn't being entirely honest with you. My boat isn't actually full of bulging treasure chests.'

The Pirate Captain was dimly aware that this was the point in the adventure where he had the opportunity to come clean, and at the risk of a slightly wounded pride he and the crew could spend the next couple of weeks just sitting about Nantucket, chewing opium and taking naps. But he looked at the smirk playing across Black Bellamy's face and he looked at Cutlass Liz's fantastic cheekbones, and somehow the confession stuck in his craw.

'The truth of the matter,' the Pirate Captain found himself saying, 'is that the treasure chests aren't on my boat. Because they're buried on one of the Cayman Islands. For tax purposes.'[8]

---

8 Legend has it that in 1788 Caymanians rescued the crews of a Jamaican merchant ship convoy which had struck a reef at Gun Bay and that they were rewarded with King George III's promise never again to impose any tax.

Black Bellamy stifled a laugh, and Cutlass Liz puffed out her cheeks and weighed up the Captain and his rag-tag crew with a steely stare.

'I wouldn't normally do this, Pirate Captain,' she finally said, 'but you have a pleasant, open face. And I like your little milk-bottle man.'

Cutlass Liz disappeared into her office for a moment.

'Lovely girl, that Cutlass,' said Black Bellamy with a wink to the Pirate Captain. 'There's something really irresistible about a woman who can kill a man with just a pork loin, don't you think?'

'Haven't you got to go and be diabolical somewhere?' replied the Captain with a grimace.

Black Bellamy grinned again and looked at his pocket watch. 'I won't take that to heart, because I know you don't mean it. And I'm sure we'll be seeing each other again soon. So, till next time then.' With a bow and a wave to all the pirates Black Bellamy sauntered back down the dock, humming a cheery little shanty to himself as he went.

When Cutlass Liz reappeared from her office she was carrying a stack of papers the size of a ship's log. She handed them to the Pirate Captain.

'You'll just need to sign this.'

The Pirate Captain leafed through the contract as his crew crowded around. 'This bit about cutting off my luxuriant beard if I default on the first payment. Is that really necessary?' said the Pirate Captain, wincing.

'And the paragraph describing how you'll hunt us down across the Seven Seas, and gut us like fishes. That seems needlessly graphic,' said the pirate with a scarf.

Cutlass Liz smiled sweetly, and waved at the array of skulls she had scattered about the boatyard. Most of them looked about the size and shape of the average pirate head.

'It's all standard terms and conditions,' she said, handing the Captain a quill which, if he didn't know better, looked as if it had been dipped in blood.

Three

I KNIFED MY WAY TO A DIAMOND PIT!

The Pirate Captain and the scarf-wearing pirate stood on the dock staring at a gigantic glass egg-timer. Cutlass Liz had been very helpful in supplying it to the pirates and making clear exactly what it was for. 'Before this runs out, you boys bring me the full balance owing,' she had said, 'otherwise I'll enact section six, paragraph four. But I will be using a harpoon instead of an axe, to add a bit of local colour.' She had also taken great pride in letting them know that the grains in the egg-timer weren't grains of sand, but pieces of ground-up pirate bones. On their way back to clear out the old boat the pirate with a scarf tried to make some small-talk about how you didn't seem to find the same quality of cannonball about nowadays, but the Pirate Captain could tell he was just trying to take his mind off their predicament.

'Feisty lass, that Cutlass Liz, isn't she, Number Two?' said the Pirate Captain, packing away his portraits in an old wooden trunk.

'You could put it like that,' said the pirate with a scarf dubiously.

'I suppose you noticed the frisson between us?' added the Pirate Captain. 'That was sexual tension. I think she was quite impressed by me.'

The pirate with a scarf nodded. The Pirate Captain was a master of understanding body language, and he often detected things that nobody else would have picked up on.

The Pirate Captain clicked the trunk shut and beckoned for a couple of the crew to take it across to the *Lovely Emma*. Then he began to flick through the boat's inventory, to make sure that nothing got left behind. It didn't make for jaunty reading:

24 limes
1 Prize Ham
18 dry cured hams
2 boxes of ship's biscuits (one set custard
   cream/one bourbon)
4 barrels of tar
5 emergency doubloons taped to the underside of
   the teapot

*I pirate with an accordion (deceased and
subsquently electroplated)*

'It *is* just possible I got a little carried away, Number Two,' he said. 'We don't actually have any loot whatsoever, do we?'

'Not really, sir. We have several limes.'

The Pirate Captain ran a concerned hand through his luxuriant beard. 'I knew I was exaggerating our finances, but I had no idea things were in quite such a sorry state.'

'We do have that big stone coin, Captain. I think that's worth something on one of the more remote Pacific island economies.'9

Whilst the crew busied themselves moving everything into the new boat, the Pirate Captain went and sat on the edge of the dock, next to the strips of gelatinous jellyfish bladders left out for salting. He whistled a little tune to himself and wondered where on earth he was going to find six thousand doubloons. A swarthy cove came and sat down next to him, and for one horrible moment the

---

9 If you are a fan of ridiculous oversized currency made out of big rolls of feathers and the like, then the Pitt Rivers Museum in Oxford is a great place to visit. Whilst you're there be sure to check out the shrunken heads that you will find downstairs in a display case next to some old violins.

Pirate Captain thought he was going to be proposi-
tioned, because a surprising amount of that sort of thing
went on amongst these sailor types. But rather than a
saucy wink or a pinch on his seafaring behind, the man
just offered him a swig of drink. He was a fearsome-
looking fellow, with an ugly scar running the length of
one cheek, and a stump of whale ivory poking out of his
trousers instead of the more regular leg. But he was
offering grog, so it seemed only right to be friendly.

'Call me Pirate Captain,' said the Pirate Captain, shaking his hand.

'Aaarrr,' said the stranger. 'The name's Ahab.'

And with that the man went back to staring at the
black waves, almost as if he was looking for something.
The Pirate Captain wasn't very good at sharing a comfortable silence with someone, unless it was a girl he
had been seeing for a while. And even then, once the
friendly feminine chatter had lapsed for too long, he
tended to babble on about how much he liked the smell
of their hair. So after a couple of awkward minutes he
tried to kick-start the conversation.

'So. Ahab. You off anywhere interesting?'

'The whale,' the man murmured. 'I'm going to find
myself the whale. I've charted the course he takes, and
I'll sail to the ends of the earth if I have to. Typhoons,
hurricanes, craggy rocks ... Why, if the sea itself rose up
against me, Ahab would not be stopped in his ungodly
quest.'

'Wow. You must really like whales.'

'Not exactly,' said Ahab, his gaze still fixed on the sea. 'It was a whale that did this,' and he pointed at his ivory leg.

'A whale made you a prosthetic leg?' exclaimed the Pirate Captain, a little incredulously. 'But how? They don't have hands, do they? Just little flippers.'

'I meant it was the whale that left me without a leg. It was a man in Bedford gave me a new one.'

'Oh. I got bitten by a mosquito once,' offered the Pirate Captain. 'Look here – you can still see the bump. Well, you can't see it now, but a week ago it was the size of a golf ball.'

'I've never forgiven the brute,' snarled Ahab. 'And I mean to hunt him down to his watery grave.'

'Well, I've never forgiven that mosquito. But you can't spend your life chasing after a mosquito, can you?'

'He was white, Pirate Captain. White as snow. And monstrous big.'

'Goodness. I'm not sure I can really remember what that mosquito looked like at all. I mean to say, I don't know if I could pick him out in some sort of identity parade.'

'I'll have my vengeance!' spat Ahab, boiling with a tremendous fury. He looked as if he was about to hit something, but seemed to settle for just pulling an angry face. After a moment the strange man slapped the Pirate Captain on the back, stood up and turned to go.

'Good hunting, Pirate Captain!' said the mysterious fellow.

'Yes, and you,' said the Pirate Captain, a bit puzzled by the whole encounter. He wandered thoughtfully back to the *Lovely Emma*.

'Are we good to go, Number Two?' asked the Pirate Captain.

'Aye aye, Captain,' said the pirate with a scarf.

'Tell me something. Do you remember that mosquito, attacked me near Mozambique?'

'Erm, no. Not really, Captain.'

'Aaarrrr, well, that will be because I was so stoic about it, I hardly made any fuss. Big brute he was. Might even have been a queen. Do mosquitos have queens?'

'I think that's bees, Pirate Captain.'

'This wasn't a bee. It was definitely a mosquito – sucked my blood right out, like a ghoul. 'Anyhow, perhaps I went a little easy on the thing?'

'You've always been the magnanimous type, Captain.'

'You don't think it makes me look soft?'

'No, sir. Gentlemanly.'

Four

A SLOW BOAT
TO BLOODSHED!

'It even comes with its own meat slicer,' said the pirate in green, flicking through the *Lovely Emma*'s brochure. 'Apparently it cuts ham so wafer-thin you can see through the slices! Imagine that! You could put ham all over your eyes and still see where you were going!'

'And it has proper beds, with mattresses!' said the albino pirate happily. 'No more falling out of stupid hammocks all the time.'

The pirates were all very excited by their new boat. Some of them thought the best thing about the *Lovely Emma* was its fancy on-board plumbing. Some of them thought the best things were the cannon covers made from ermine and pressed swans. Some of them thought the best thing was the ornamental garden. The Captain thought the best thing was probably the huge network of speaking tubes that ran around the length of the boat, because it meant he could talk to the crew or sing them a shanty whenever he felt like it, even if it was in the middle of the night. But whatever the best thing about the boat was, the pirates all agreed that the *Lovely Emma* was brilliant.

In his brand-new office the Pirate Captain pressed a button under his brand-new desk and watched as a shiny mahogany cupboard slid open. A little wooden monkey poured out a cup of grog and then did a clumsy mechanical dance, before disappearing back inside the cupboard. The Pirate Captain chuckled, drank the grog and then pressed the button over and over again, so that it looked like the wooden monkey was having an epileptic fit. He had just finally broken the monkey when the pirate in green came in with his afternoon tea.

'Tea, Captain,' said the pirate in green.

'Lovely,' said the Pirate Captain. 'Grog is all well and good, but it doesn't really beat a nice cup of tea.'

The pirate in green started to pour it out, but his hands were shaking and he ended up spilling most of the tea over the Captain's desk.

'Sorry, Captain. I'm not myself,' said the pirate in green, wiping the mess up with his sleeve.

'Something on your mind?'

'Don't get me wrong, Captain. It's great to have a nice new boat. It's just a couple of us pirates were thinking six thousand doubloons is an awful lot of money for us to come by in one adventure. And the getting cut to bits business ... I don't much fancy the sound of that.'

'You know something?' said the Pirate Captain. 'For a moment there I would have agreed with you. It occurred to me that I might have been a touch rash saddling us with such a large debt. But sat here, looking at the way all this wood panelling brings out the russet hues of my beard, I've realised that *not* to have bought this boat would have been *false economy*. And you know what I'm always saying – the pirate's worst enemy is false economy. Even more so than the Royal Navy.'

Because the pirate in green didn't have the Pirate Captain's firm grasp of economics, he wasn't sure he understood the exact way in which false economy worked, but he vaguely remembered that it tended to crop up a lot when the Pirate Captain was shopping for meat and fancied treating himself to something from the butcher's *Finest* range.

'Besides, she looks a lot happier there, doesn't she?' said the Pirate Captain, nodding at his Prize Ham, which was now hung proudly in its case above the fireplace.

'She definitely goes very well with the lush carpeting,' agreed the pirate in green.

'Have I ever told you how I first came across the old dear?'

In fact the Pirate Captain had told the pirates his Prize Ham's origin story on several occasions, though it seemed to change every time. Depending on the Captain's mood the ham was either: an offering from a dying Aztec king; stolen from inside the tomb of a pharaoh; won in a duel with a samurai; the reincarnation of a gypsy princess; or a Christmas present from his Aunt Joan. The pirate in green was actually rather relieved that before the Pirate Captain could elaborate any further the sensible tones of the pirate with a scarf came wafting down the speaking tube to tell them that there was something up on deck that they should see.

For a moment after bounding up onto the deck the Pirate Captain wasn't sure what it was that the pirate with a scarf had called him for, but then he looked up and saw the thing.

'Oooh! An albatross! I think they're supposed to be lucky, aren't they?' said the Pirate Captain, squinting up at the majestic bird which was flying in little circles around the mast.

'Actually, sir, the albatross is traditionally seen as a symbol of oppressive burden or hindrance,' said the pirate in red.[10] It was a credit to the Captain's self-control that the pirate in red didn't get a cutlass in his eye right there and then.

'It has something tied to its leg, Captain.'

'So it has. What do you suppose it could be?'

'Perhaps it's a treasure map!'

---

10 The albatross can live for up to eighty years, and it has the largest wingspan of any bird, often exceeding eleven and a half feet.

'Let's throw our cutlasses at it!' said the Pirate Captain.

A few of the pirates threw their cutlasses at the albatross, but it easily swooped out of the way, the cutlasses clattered back onto the deck and everybody had to scatter to avoid getting run through. Jennifer muttered something about how the Pirate Captain ought to think his plans through a little more. The Pirate Captain looked up at the albatross and narrowed his eyes.

'We're going to have to lure it down here somehow,' he said, a wily look coming over his face. 'One of you lubbers go fetch me some hens from the kitchen.'

The sassy pirate drew the short straw and he was soon rolling around in a puddle of pirate tar. Then all the other pirates took turns to throw some freshly plucked hen feathers at him, until he was covered from head to toe. He got a bit cross because a few of the feathers went in his mouth. Then the pirate who was good at origami folded his scarf into the shape of a beak, and they attached it with a rubber band to the sassy pirate's face. Jennifer fetched her lipstick and drew a lovely pair of sexy lady albatross lips on the sassy pirate's new beak. The sassy pirate already had naturally long eyelashes like a girl, so they didn't need to do anything with those.

'Make some sexy albatross noises,' said the Pirate Captain. 'And flap your arms a bit.'

The sassy pirate clearly didn't know what a sexy lady albatross sounded like, but he did his best. 'Caw! Caw!' he said through his origami scarf-beak. 'I'm a sexy lady albatross!'

It did the trick, and the other – genuine – albatross flapped down towards him, a frisky look in its avian eye. But before the lusty bird could put any albatross moves on the sassy pirate, the Pirate Captain leapt forward and covered it with a big sack. A few cutlass prods and some squawking later and the albatross lay dead on the floor.

'Look, Captain! It was a lady albatross all along!'

'Well. Who's to say albatrosses can't enjoy a touch of the Sapphic?' said the Pirate Captain reasonably. The crew all crowded around as the pirate with a scarf slipped a soggy piece of parchment from the bird's leg.

'Here's a stroke of luck!' said the Pirate Captain. 'It's a letter from Calico Jack, my old mentor at pirate academy.'

The Pirate Captain began to read the letter out loud:

'Dear Pirate Captain,
I hope all is well and that you're not hanging in irons or anything. I'm writing to you from my sickbed, where I am suffering terribly with a kidney stone the size of a grape-fruit. Such a common risk for us pirates, given our fondness for rich meats of all descriptions.' [11]

---

[11] Kidney stones are a conglomeration of crystals (called calculi) in the kidney and bladder, which are exacerbated by high levels of uric acid. Meat, rhubarb, spinach, cocoa, pepper, nuts and tea have been linked with stone formation, as well as insufficient intake of fluids.

Several of the crew shook their heads sadly, and more than one made a mental note to cut back on the feasts.

'I fear that my days of plundering and shouting things like 'I am a pirate!' may well be drawing to a close. So I wanted to tell you one thing — Pirate Captain, you were always my favourite pupil. Certainly you were much better than the others in your class, who I regarded merely as a brain, an athlete, a basket case, a princess and a criminal. I especially liked your commanding voice, stentorian nose, piercing blue eyes and firm grasp of nautical matters.

Even as I write I can feel additional calculi agglomerating in my urinary tract, so I must be brief. Long story short, I believe that you, more than anybody, deserve to learn my greatest secret: for as a young pirate I discovered nothing less than the <u>ultimate treasure</u>, which I buried for safe-keeping on an island just off the Florida Keys. The map is enclosed.

Stay lucky,
Calico Jack.' [12]

'Does the letter really say all that about you having a commanding voice and piercing eyes?' said the pirate in red, peering over the Pirate Captain's shoulder. 'I can't see that bit anywhere.'

---

12 A letter like this would probably have been known as a 'booty call'.

The Pirate Captain glowered at the pirate in red, rolled up the letter and put it in his pocket. He turned to his second-in-command and grinned.

'You see? You worry too much. I told you something would come up.'

The pirates were all excited by what the ultimate treasure might turn out to be. The albino pirate thought that it would probably be the world's biggest necklace, whilst the pirate in green thought it would be a diamond so massive you couldn't even fit it into your mouth, and a few of the others were convinced it would be One Million Pounds.

'Whatever it turns out to be,' said the Pirate Captain, trying to calm his crew down a bit, 'it's sure to be enough to pay for the boat, and keep us in hooks and buckles for years to come. And if there's any left over, well, you know me ... I'll probably give it to charity. Amputee pirates. Or maybe to some sort of creature sanctuary. You've got to give something back, haven't you?'

The pirates all nodded solemnly.

'Don't just stand about, lads. Brace the jib and hoist the mainsail and – uh – do all those things that make the boat go,' said the Pirate Captain, striding towards his office. 'With any luck, by this time tomorrow we'll be drinking champagne[13] from the smalls of ladies' backs!

---

13 During the early nineteenth century, up to forty per cent of champagne bottles exploded before even leaving the vineyard.

Except for Jennifer, of course. You can drink champagne from the small of a beefcake's back. Well, not just Jennifer, any of you can if you go for that sort of thing. I'm open-minded like that.'

The pirates had been digging for hours. Their muscles ached and the sweat streamed in torrents down their backs and faces. The stinging tropical sun rendered them speechless.

'You're doing a great job, lads!' said the Pirate Captain, sat a little way away under a stylish skull-and-crossbones parasol. He washed down a slice of ham with a swig of pirate grog. 'I just wish I could help. But you know what happens when I get sand in my beard – I could be out of action for days.'

The pirate in red wiped a soggy neckerchief across his brow and leant on his spade for a moment. 'Are you sure this is the spot, Captain?' he asked.

'Yes. Can't be long now! Chop, chop!' said the Pirate Captain, trying to be firm.

'You've got the treasure map the right way round this time?'

The Pirate Captain was a little annoyed that the pirate in red should have brought this up again.

'Aarrrr. This is definitely the place – see, Old Jack marked that the treasure was next to a shrub which looked like the rude part of a lady.' He pointed at the map and then at the shrub that was shaped just like a woman's bare ankle. A couple of the pirates giggled and nudged each other.

'I know it's hard work, me beauties, but it's going to be worth it!'

Much to the Pirate Captain's relief, before any further discussion could take place there came the unmistakable clank of spade against wood.

'Hooray!' yelled the sassy pirate. 'I found a treasure chest!'

With a new surge of energy, the crew hefted an antique chest up onto the sand.

'The ultimate treasure!' said the Pirate Captain, a little embarrassed to actually find himself salivating at the prospect. He wiped a big bit of slobber away with his sleeve. 'This is pay day, lads!' he added, after a suitably dramatic pause.

As the Pirate Captain forced the rusty hinges with his cutlass, the crew backed away a little just in case a mummy or a zombie pirate should jump out, because it wouldn't be the first time. But instead of a mummy or a zombie pirate there was just a solitary picture of a grinning child with a brief note scrawled on the back of it.

Isn't the ultimate treasure a child's smile? Isn't a drop of rain on the wing of a butterfly worth a million doubloons?
Yours, Calico Jack

'Oh,' said the Pirate Captain, biting his lip. 'Isn't that nice?'

Somewhere a parrot squawked.

'Yes,' said the pirate with a scarf, who looked like he was about to burst into tears. 'And it's so true. When you think about it.'

'We've learnt an important lesson today about what's really valuable,' said the pirate in green through clenched teeth.

The pirates spent the next few minutes avoiding each other's gaze and saying how this was much better than the ultimate treasure turning out to be something predictable like jewels or gold. Calico Jack's message so impressed the albino pirate that he kicked the head off one of the baby seals that were mucking about on the beach. The crew reluctantly picked up their spades and hats and trudged silently back to where the *Lovely Emma* was parked.

Eventually the Pirate Captain couldn't help himself. 'I'm not saying I'm not richer in spirit or anything,' he said, 'but it would have been nice if there'd been a bit of booty in there as well.'

The pirate crew all started talking at once.

'All that digging and not a single bloody diamond!'

'The wing of a butterfly? A *butterfly*?'

'Calico Spack, more like!'

Five

SATAN'S FISH ATE
US ALIVE!

'Well, lads, you'll be happy to know I have a new plan,' said the Pirate Captain, striking his most businesslike pose. The pirate crew, who were all sprawled on one of the *Lovely Emma*'s tennis courts awaiting their Captain's idea, gazed up at him expectantly.

'We're going,' said the Pirate Captain, a glint in his eye, 'to Las Vegas!'

The pirates all looked at each other in surprise. It wasn't exactly the announcement they had been anticipating.

'Las Vegas?'

'That's right. Las Vegas. The city of dreaming spires.'

'But you're always saying how gambling is terrible,

Pirate Captain. You said it was even worse than calling people names.'

'But then we had that adventure where you wagered the whole boat and crew that nobody could beat you at thumb-wrestling.'

'Which is it, Pirate Captain?' said the albino pirate. 'Is gambling terrible or good?'

'We are not,' said the Pirate Captain, 'going to Vegas to gamble.'

'Oh. Why *are* we going? Is it the whoring?'

'No, it's not that either. Come on, you lubbers – what else is Las Vegas famous for?'

The pirate crew gave a collective shrug.

'Showbusiness! You know how good I am at telling anecdotes. And we're always having adventures. It's just the sort of place an entertaining act such as ourselves could be a hit.'

The pirates wriggled uncomfortably from foot to foot. A couple of them tapped their heads meaningfully.

'Come on!' bellowed the Pirate Captain. 'It was bound to come down to this sooner or later. Why are you all looking so put out?'

'It's just ... I don't think we realised you had ambitions in that particular direction,' said the pirate with a scarf.

'It's not just one of my fads, if that's what you mean.'

'Are you sure about this, Captain?' said the pirate in red.

'I do have a sensitive side, you know,' said the Pirate Captain with a pout. 'I realise you lot tend to think I'm just about the hair and the grisly murder, but that's simply not the case. You might be surprised to hear that sometimes I enjoy taking a little time out to read Shakespeare, and make daisy chains, and artistic stuff like that. I've always felt a certain calling for the stage. In many ways I think that's why I got into piracy in the first place, because it's quite dramatic.'

'Sorry, Captain,' said the pirate in green. 'I hope you haven't felt too misunderstood all these years.'

'Aaarrr, that's okay. It's a lonely job, being a Pirate Captain. I knew that when I signed on.'

The crew were pretty tired by the time the *Lovely Emma* arrived in Las Vegas[14], because even though this adventure was taking place in America, they still had to sail across Texas and half of Nevada. There was a hair-raising encounter along the way with a shoal of box jellyfish, which washed up onto the deck during a typhoon, and the Pirate Captain had to make sure the crew were all wearing their pirate shoes: 'Something you should do anyway,' he pointed out, 'because of verrucas.' The pirates had then spent an enjoyable afternoon running around the boat smacking the jellyfish with spades.

---

14 In 1829 Santa Fe merchant Antonio Armijo led a party on the Old Spanish Trail to Los Angeles. When they discovered an abundance of artesian water in a valley, they named it 'Las Vegas', Spanish for 'the Fertile Valley'.

Luckily for the pirates the Las Vegas of those days was a lawless place, so just for once they didn't have to disguise themselves as washerwomen or scientists or anything like that to avoid getting arrested. In fact, life in the American Wild West was really a lot like life on the High Seas. Obviously there were a few minor differences, but these were pretty superficial – it was mostly a matter of certain things being known by different names. The pirate with a scarf gave out a list to the rest of the crew, just to avoid any confusion whilst they were there:

The High Seas		The American Wild West
Pirates	=	Cowboys
Walking the plank	=	Lynchings
Exotic Palm Trees	=	Cacti
Sharks	=	Rattlesnakes
Ham	=	Jerky
Roaring	=	Whooping
Shanties	=	Campfire songs
Lubbers	=	Varmints
Rip-roaring adventure	=	Hornswoggling adventure
Jellyfish	=	Coyotes

The crew all dutifully memorised their lists, parked the boat in a lake next to some cowboy wagons, and went to have a look about the place. The pirates were very excited by the Las Vegas buildings, which were in the shape of buildings that you wouldn't expect to find in the middle of the desert. The Pirate Captain tried to look nonchalant, because he didn't want to undermine the world-weary been-there-done-that image he liked to cultivate, but it wasn't easy because he was almost as excited as the men.

'Look at that one,' said the pirate in green. 'It's like a real medieval castle! Like we have in England!'

'That one's shaped like a pyramid!'

'And that one's shaped like a *pirate boat*!'

The pirates couldn't help but gawp at all the bright lights and the glamorous people walking down the strip. The prevalent fashion in Las Vegas appeared to be ten-gallon hats and handlebar moustaches for the men and 'almost bare' for the ladies.

The pirates all looked with big longing eyes at one of the glittering casinos. And then they all looked with big pleading eyes at their Captain. A few of them started to bounce up and down on the spot, which was always a sure sign that they were getting overexcited.

'Please, Pirate Captain!' said the pirate with rickets.

'*Please*,' said the pirate with gout.

'We could get one of those almost bare ladies to blow on our dice with real lady breath,' said the pirate in red.

'I heard it's impossible to lose when they do that!' said the pirate with a nut allergy.

'Snake eyes!' shouted the albino pirate. He wasn't sure what it meant, but he wanted to join in.

The Pirate Captain sighed. 'I suppose it wouldn't be the end of the world. And besides, let's not forget that last adventure we had in a casino,' he added, winking at his second-in-command. 'There's always the chance that some bored millionaire type will offer me a fortune to let him spend one night with the pirate with a scarf.'

The pirates headed straight for the roulette[15] table, because it had a big shiny spinning wheel on it, and just like magpies pirates tend to find themselves drawn to shiny things.[16]

The pirates tried to decide if it was best putting their doubloons on black or on red. Half of the pirates argued that it was best to put them on black, because that was the colour of their sturdy pirate boots. And the other half thought it was best to put them on red, because that was the colour of blood, and they wanted to show that they were a murderous bunch. In the end they compromised and put their doubloons on the little green zero, because that was the colour of rolling fields back in England, and they were all feeling a little homesick.

---

15 Blackbeard is said to have invented a game he called 'Pirate Roulette'. When he was very bored he would lock himself in the hold with his crew and let off a volley of random shots with his pistol. Then he would count how many dead pirates there were.

16 Barracudas, sometimes known as the 'Tigers of the Sea', are also a lot like magpies, as they are attracted to shiny reflective things, which has led to a number of attacks on necklace-wearers.

Ten minutes later, having lost not only the emergency doubloons taped to the bottom of the teapot but also the teapot itself, the pirates were starting to think that perhaps the Pirate Captain had been right in the first place, and that maybe gambling wasn't so great after all. They decided to go and play on the slot machines with their last few pieces of eight.

'I think it's obvious that table was rigged, Pirate Captain,' said the pirate in green.

'And I didn't like the look of that croupier. Did you notice that he had no ear lobes? I remember hearing that's a sure sign of dishonesty in a man,' said the pirate with gout.

'Don't be too disheartened, lads,' said the Pirate Captain. 'After all, you're forgetting the actual reason we're here. We've come to put on a show!' To illustrate the point he did a little tap-dance while holding an imaginary cane, and in the process accidentally bumped into an elderly man who was sat at one of the slot machines a little way along. The man let out a muffled curse, and his leg clattered onto the floor.

'Oh good grief! I've knocked your leg off! I'm so sorry!' said the Pirate Captain, stricken. 'I don't know my own strength sometimes.'

It was then he noticed that the leg which was lying on the floor wasn't a normal-looking leg, but a chunk of glinting whalebone. He looked up to see a scowling face with a livid scar that he recognised as belonging to the friendly stranger from Nantucket docks.

'Ahab! It is Ahab, isn't it?' said the Captain.

'Pirate Captain,' said Ahab.

The Pirate Captain handed Ahab his leg back.

'Thank you,' said Ahab, and then he rather joylessly turned back to the slot machine.

'Fancy seeing you here! I thought you were off looking for that whale.'

Ahab turned a sullen eye on the Captain. 'Aye, Pirate Captain. Ahab does not rest. Some of my whaler crew told me that the white fiend had been sighted here.'

'Really? Here in the desert? Not the usual habitat, is it?'

'He is a mighty devious beast, Captain.'

'I suppose he must be,' said the Pirate Captain thoughtfully.

'The men informed me that they had seen the whale entering into this very casino. Gambling is a filthy vice, as I'm sure you would agree, but one I find not in the least surprising from a creature so lacking in honest virtue.'

There was a sharp pinging sound from Ahab's slot machine, and a pile of shiny doubloons poured out onto the old whaler's lap. The Pirate Captain looked at them wistfully.

'Ahab seems to have got three lemons,' said Ahab. He scooped up his winnings and heaved a weary sigh. 'But what is money to me? Only cold revenge can soothe a soul such as mine.'

'Yes, cold revenge sounds good. Or maybe you should go and take in a show,' suggested the Pirate Captain with a hopeful grin. 'It just so happens that me and the lads here are planning on putting on a bit of a perform-ance ourselves. I'm sure you'd enjoy it, and it may take your mind off the whaling for a while.'

'I am sorry, Captain. I have no time for such things,' said Ahab, screwing his whalebone leg back into place and getting up from his stool. 'And the beast appears to have given me the slip once more, so if you'll excuse me, Ahab must take his leave.'

And with a brisk nod of his well-weathered head, Ahab stalked out of the casino.

'Are all your friends that dour, Captain?' asked the pirate with a hook for a hand as the pirates wandered back to the *Lovely Emma*.

'Only the ones racked with eternal torment,' explained the Captain. 'The rest are pretty frivolous.'

The pirates quickly busied themselves making a little stage out of some barrels and planks of wood from the boat's lumber room. They used one of her sails to make a theatrical curtain and put out deckchairs at the front for the audience. Meanwhile the Pirate Captain locked himself up in his office with a broad selection of coloured pens, scissors and glue. When he eventually

came out he was looking pretty pleased with himself.
He unfurled a huge banner:

THE PIRATE CAPTAIN PRESENTS:
A CAVALCADE OF CUTLASS CAPERS!

···

Featuring:

The PIRATE CAPTAIN recounting
his best anecdotes (both nautical
and land-based)!
Jennifer (an actual lady) throwing knifes!
The tallest pirate on the Seven Seas!
Pirates doing rousing shanties!
The PIRATE CAPTAIN's moving
monologues!
An albino that walks like a man!
And divers other entertainments,
culminating in the grand finale, where
the PIRATE CAPTAIN will knock out a
ferocious lion with a single punch!

'What do you think, lads?'

'I like the alliteration, Pirate Captain,' said the pirate
with a scarf.

'Yes,' said the Pirate Captain proudly. 'I thought of
doing it with Ks – you know, Kavalcade of Kutlass
Kapers. But then I thought that might be a bit much.'

'I can see that,' said the pirate with a scarf. 'Are you really going to knock out a ferocious lion?'

'Not as such. Well, *no*. I might have been embellishing.'

After the pirates had hung the banner over the back of the *Lovely Emma* and had gone round the dusty little town handing out a few flyers, the Pirate Captain decided it was time to rehearse.

'Right, lads, let's get this show on the road! I thought we'd start by workshopping a few scenes – you know, to get a feel of our roles.'

'Erm ... I was just going to do a couple of shanties, to be honest,' said the pirate in green. 'I was thinking educational for the matinee and a little more bawdy in the evening.'

'That sounds good,' said the Pirate Captain. 'What about you, Jennifer? How's the knife-throwing coming along?'

'Oh, I've not really tried it yet,' said Jennifer airily. 'But it can't be that hard, can it? It's only knifes after all. Just to be on the safe side, I thought I'd use the pirate with a peg-leg as my partner, seeing as he's already so used to losing bits and pieces.'

Jennifer smiled at the pirate with a peg-leg. The pirate with a peg-leg looked a bit miserable.

The pirate in green went round the audience with his hat to collect the night's takings. Just about all of Wild West life was there – millionaires, cowboys, native Americans, and even a few women of ill-repute. He knew that the people in Vegas had a bit of a reputation, so when he was collecting the doubloons he bit down on them, because he had seen people do this before, but he wasn't sure why, because all he could tell was that it made his fillings hurt.

Behind the curtain the Pirate Captain was doing a few stretching exercises and going over his lines.

'Now. Do you think I should do the mosquito anecdote?'

'I should say the shark anecdote is better, Captain,' replied the scarf-wearing pirate.

'It occurred to me, as some sort of framing device, I might explain the story behind each of my scars.'

'That's a good idea, Captain.'

'This nasty one here? That's the time I had my BCG.'

'Yes, Captain. I remember the nurse said you were very brave.'

'I think the rest are all from slipping over in the bath.'

'The ocean certainly is a rocky mistress.'

The scarf-wearing pirate gave the sassy pirate a nod,

the sassy pirate tugged on a rope and up went the makeshift curtain.

'Hello Las Vegas!' said the Pirate Captain, waving to the audience with both hands. 'It's lovely to be here!'

The show got off to an energetic start, with all the pirates doing a shanty about swimming really fast. Next up was the tallest pirate on the Seven Seas, who came on and did a little dance to the sound of an accordion. The tallest pirate on the Seven Seas was wearing a very long coat and had a normal-sized head that looked a lot like the pirate in green's head. When the tallest pirate on the Seven Seas left the stage to a polite round of applause he nearly fell over as his top half turned to bow to the audience and his bottom half continued into the wings.[17] Then there was some tumbling from some of the more lively pirates and after that the Pirate Captain invited a few children up onto the stage. He magicked some eggs from behind their ears, sat them all on a bench and got them to sing a jolly shanty about the harsh life of a pirate. The Pirate Captain warned them that the theatre was haunted and that they had to keep singing – even if a scary ghost came and touched their shoulder. As the

---

17 The tallest man ever was Robert Wadlow, standing 8' 11" in his stockinged feet. He was medically a giant – a condition caused by an excess of growth hormone. Tall stature is accompanied by broad, spade-like fingers, over-developed jaw and cheekbones and a disproportionately large skull.

children sang, the albino pirate sneaked on and chased them off one by one, until only the littlest kid was left, absolutely terrified out of his wits, whilst the Pirate Captain chuckled away. Then the Pirate Captain told him that it was all okay and that the ghost was actually just an albino. He let the littlest kid feed the albino a couple of pieces of meringue to see how harmless he was. Then the Pirate Captain sang a shanty to the kid about how we have to look after the children, because they are our future. The show finished with the Pirate Captain's moving environmental monologue that he had entitled 'The Last Dolphin In The Sea'. It was a bit downbeat, because he had written it when he was in a mood and it had been raining, but the pirates all agreed that the environment was a serious matter and needed to be treated as such. Halfway through the monologue the accordion broke, but fortunately the pirate with asthma was on hand to step up and do 'human accordion', which was a bit like human beatbox, but with more emphasis on wheezing.

> '. . . where are my friends,
> Oh where can they be?
> Life is so lonely when you're
> The last dolphin in the sea!'

'Remember. There's magic inside each and every one of you. Never forget that,' said the Pirate Captain, wiping a tear from his cheek and bowing to the audience as the curtain came down. All the pirates were buzzing.

'That went brilliantly, Captain!' said the pirate with a scarf, clutching a big bag of the evening's takings. He'd drawn a big thermometer to show how close they were getting to the six thousand doubloons and he set about colouring in the current total.

'It did go well, didn't it?' said the Captain, dabbing at his forehead with a handkerchief. 'I think I was born to the stage, lads. This is my calling. If you cut me, do I not bleed greasepaint?'

'I'm sure that during our adventure with a circus you said you had sawdust in your veins, Captain.'

'Aaarrr. Yes. Also greasepaint. Sawdust and greasepaint.'

'That must make a sort of gooey paste, Captain.'

Six

DEATH FEAST OF THE PANTHER WOMEN!

'... So I said to him, "Larry – you can't go on like that, you just *can't*!" '

The Pirate Captain was regaling the pirates with a theatrical anecdote.

'And do you know what? He bloody did! He went on and *bloody stormed it*. Great times, lads. Great times.'

The pirates all sighed and shook their heads at Larry. Since the night before, the Pirate Captain had become an even better raconteur than ever, with a ready supply of funny and moving tales from the wonderful world of showbusiness.

'Five-minute call, Mr Captain!' shouted the pirate with a strawberry birthmark, and the pirates started scurrying about for the second night's performance. The Pirate Captain took a moment to tease his eyebrows into points. He stopped to look approvingly at himself in a mirror.

'ME ME ME. MO MO MO. MA MA MA,' he said to his reflection. The pirate in green straightened his hat for him. 'They're pretty quiet out there, Captain,' said the pirate in green.

'I expect they're trembling in anticipation. They'll have been looking forward to it all day.'

The Pirate Captain closed his eyes, took a deep breath and bounded onto the stage.

'Laaaadies and Gentlemen! Live on stage, fresh from the Seven Seas, it is *I*, the Pirate Captain! Raarggh!'

He waited for the applause. And he waited. After a bit more waiting he opened his eyes. There was nobody there. Just row upon row of empty deckchairs.[18]

'You can come out,' said the Pirate Captain. 'I'm not really that terrifying!'

'I don't understand it, Captain,' said the pirate with a hook for a hand, as they wandered disconsolately down one of Las Vegas's brightly lit streets.

'The reviews felt you were a "powerhouse of perform-ance",' said the pirate in green.

---

18 Deckchairs can be quite dangerous – the Portuguese dictator Antonio de Oliveira Salazar suffered a fatal heart attack after getting himself entangled in a deckchair.

'Fame is fickle,' said the scarf-wearing pirate wisely.

The Pirate Captain shook his head. 'It doesn't make any sense, lads. Yesterday we were all the rage, and now we can't shift a single ticket. It's a mystery.'

He took out the pirate with a scarf's useful table from a pocket and grumpily doodled an extra couple of columns:

The High Seas (pirates)	The Wild West (cowboys)
Pushes theatrical boundaries	Lack of artistic vision
Brilliant hats	Rubbish hats

He was just about to add a third column about how much better his removable shiny pirate boots were compared to the dirty old cowboy boots that cowboys couldn't take off when, with a *tap tap tapping* sound, who should they spot but Ahab hurrying down the dusty street.

'Hello Ahab,' the Pirate Captain called out. 'Any joy? Whale-wise, I mean?'

Ahab hobbled sternly towards them. 'Ill-fortune besets me as ever, Captain. The leviathan has eluded me once again – the men tell me he must have slipped out the back of the casino just as we arrived.'

'He's a tricky so-and-so, isn't he?' said the Pirate Captain. 'You wouldn't expect something that big to be so stealthy, would you? Considering he's got no legs.'

Ahab glowered. 'I could spend an afternoon telling you tales of the beast's monstrous cunning, Pirate Captain. But I have an appointment to keep, so I cannot stop and chit-chat.'

'Oh, off anywhere interesting?'

'I am visiting a theatre show.'

The pirates were a little put out by this. 'I thought you said you were too busy to go to see shows?' said the pirate with a scarf.

'Ahab is a solemn fellow,' said Ahab. 'I take no pleasure from playacting. But the men insisted that after the white whale left the casino, they spotted him buying tickets for a show. This, apparently, was his choice.'

Ahab handed the Pirate Captain a theatrical flyer. The Pirate Captain's beetling brows almost leapt off his face.

'Hell's teeth! The *rogue*!'

For there, printed in a gothic pirate script above a picture of a boat, they read:

**BLACK BELLAMY IS PROUD TO PRESENT:
'A BOISTEROUS BOUT OF BUCCANEERS!'**

𝔉eaturing:

**BLACK BELLAMY APPEARING
LIVE ON STAGE**

𝔅ack by popular demand, the most famous
pirate on the 𝔖even 𝔖eas recounts tales both
thought-provoking and side-splitting about life
at sea and encounters with sea monsters, eels etc.

𝔆lassy opera singing!

𝔇ancing 𝔆ossack pirates!

𝔐agical sawing people in half with cutlasses!

**IT'S A KRAZY KASCADE OF KOMEDY,
KONVERSATION AND KRYING**

'So that's why nobody came to our show!' exclaimed the
pirate in green.

'It's almost as if he does this sort of thing just to cause
us mischief!' said the pirate in red.

'Whilst I have no time for such fripperies, one must admit that it's very clever how they've done all those Ks, do you not think, Pirate Captain?' said Ahab.

The Pirate Captain was so angry that he didn't even stop to buy popcorn before he, Ahab and the pirates burst into Black Bellamy's show. Black Bellamy was already up on stage, halfway through taking questions about cuisine from a girl from the audience who was sat on his knee.

'What's the bounciest meat in the world?' asked the girl.

'Good question,' said Black Bellamy. 'There isn't actually a bounciest meat in the world, but the chewiest meat is beef jerky, which comes from dry cows.'

'I see no sign of the accursed sea-beast,' said Ahab, scanning the auditorium, 'but my godforsaken crew are obviously enjoying themselves,' he added bitterly, looking at his whalers sat in the front row. Ahab paused, and turned to the pirates. 'You might say that they are having a whale of a time.'

The pirates looked at Ahab. There was an embarrassed silence.

'That was a joke,' said Ahab. 'Whale of a time. You see?'

The pirates went on looking at Ahab.

'I rarely make jokes,' said Ahab, a little sadly. 'I don't really have the delivery.'

Black Bellamy had finished with his question-and-answer session, and now he had begun to recount a story about the time he had disguised himself as Admiral Nelson and sunk Napoleon's flagship.

'It's funny, it's moving and it's educational,' whispered one of the audience to their neighbour.

'Much better than that other pirate last night. Much classier.'

'And I like the way his beard goes right up to his eyes.'

The Pirate Captain was just about to tap the fellow on the shoulder and point out that Black Bellamy was just an old ham, by which he certainly did not mean the good kind of mouth-watering old ham, when there was another wild round of applause.

'Thank you very much, ladies and gentlemen,' said Black Bellamy, waving for them to calm down. 'I'm now going to sing you a shanty that is very close to my heart. As you know, I care a great deal about the environment . . . This one is called "The Last Dolphin In The Sea".'

'Oh, honestly!' cried the Pirate Captain. 'That really is the final straw! Excuse me, Ahab.' And with that the Pirate Captain charged up through the audience and onto the stage.

'Hello Pirate Captain,' said Black Bellamy in a laconic voice. 'Fancy seeing you here.'

'Don't you "hello" me,' said the Pirate Captain, waggling

his cutlass. 'You're stealing my material, you cove!'

'Pirate Captain! I don't even know how to begin to respond to such a baseless accusation.'

The Pirate Captain drew himself up to his full height of five feet and nine inches. 'I've had enough, you swab. We're going to settle this in the time-honoured pirate fashion!'

'Cutlasses?' shouted a helpful audience member.

'Pistols maybe?' shouted another excitedly.

'Wrestling naked in front of a roaring log fire?'

'Is it something to do with eating?'

'No,' said the Pirate Captain, turning to the audience. 'We're going to have a shanty battle. *Mano-a-mano*, with only our voices and ready wit as weapons! What do you say, Black Bellamy?'

'Why not?' roared Black Bellamy.

The audience cheered as the pirate with the accordion began to play a simple hornpipe. The Pirate Captain tapped his foot a few times.

'Walking with my big pirate boots on the deck,
Here comes the Pirate Captain with my broad neck,
I sing with confidence, finesse and flair,
My clothes are the best and so is my hair!'

The crew and audience joined in on a chorus of 'Yo ho hos' and the Pirate Captain fixed Black Bellamy with a challenging eye. Black Bellamy swaggered confidently to the front of the stage.

'When admirals cry into their pillows at night,
It's Black Bellamy who caused their terrible plight!
I've plundered all of the Seven Seas and more,
Get out of my way when you hear me roar!'

As the crowd sang the chorus, Black Bellamy did a special backwards walk that looked as if his feet were walking forwards. The Pirate Captain stepped up.

'I move across the stage with sinuous grace,
Singing all the while from my pleasant, open face,
This Black Bellamy's show is a useless waste,
And if you think otherwise then you have no taste!'

On the last line, the Pirate Captain pointed an accusing finger at the audience and was met with a chorus of markedly less enthusiastic yo ho hos.

'The only thing more famous than my piratical
  crimes,
Is the super quality of my amazing rhymes
You try your hardest, but your shanties are jokes,
And then you insult these stand-up folks!'

Black Bellamy gestured to the crowd, who nodded and glared at the Pirate Captain. The Pirate Captain puffed out his chest.

'Only idiots couldn't see that you're a fraud.
I should have expected this from people abroad!
They're vulgar and crass and ...'

'I don't think they appreciated you saying that about their mothers, Captain,' said the pirate with a scarf as they sprinted down the street a few minutes later.

'You may be right, Number Two,' said the Pirate Captain, using his cutlass to knock aside a bottle that was aimed at his head.

'It's been a while since we've had an angry mob after us, hasn't it, Captain?' said the pirate in green.

'Not since the adventure with the Catholic girls' school!' said the pirate with long legs.

'I feel a bit bad about Ahab.'

'You mean his leg snapping off? I'm sure he's got lots of spares.'

'Yes, I suppose being trampled by furious cowboys would be nothing compared to having your leg bitten off by a whale.'

'I've decided that showbusiness isn't really for me,' said the Pirate Captain, trying to remember where they had left the boat.

'It's a bit shallow, Captain,' agreed the pirate with a hook for a hand.

'Exactly,' said the Pirate Captain. 'The public aren't really ready for my material. It may be that I'm one of those innovative types who are doomed to only be appreciated by future generations.'

Seven

AT THE COURT
OF THE CRABS!

'Next morning, after a terrible dream involving Cutlass Liz and his beard and a big pair of rusty scissors, the Pirate Captain woke to the sound of bits of pirate bones trickling through the egg-timer. He tramped bleary-eyed into the boat's breakfast room. Usually he would have expected to find it full of the merry sounds of pirates staging little naval battles, with their cornflakes as tiny galleons and the milk as the sea, and the sizzle of bacon as distant cannon fire, but today he was greeted only by a restrained munching.

'Ka-boom!' said the Pirate Captain, as he sat down and spooned some cereal into his mouth, pretending it was Royal Navy boats and that his mouth was a big whirlpool.

'Hooray! Take that Royal Navy!' a couple of the crew replied, but more than a little half-heartedly.

The Pirate Captain scratched glumly at his bushy eyebrows. 'Number Two,' he said to the pirate with a scarf. 'As soon as these breakfast things have been cleared away, I want us to make sail for Nantucket.'

'What about the six thousand doubloons?' asked the albino pirate, not able to look the Captain in the eye.[19]

'Aaarrr,' said the Pirate Captain. 'We just have to face it, lads – I'm not going to be able to raise the cash in time. I've given it my best shot. We're going to have to hand back the boat.' The men stared at their plates. 'Besides, there's always a chance Cutlass Liz will decide that a stern telling-off would be a lot less bother than all that messy murdering,' the Captain added unconvincingly.

'Can't give up now, sir,' said the pirate with rickets. A few of the pirates whispered to each other and then the albino pirate held up a little bag.

'We've had a bit of a whip-round, Captain,' he said, passing it rather shyly across the table. The Pirate Captain tipped the bag out next to his plate. It contained:

- *3 pieces of eight*
- *Some foreign coins*
- *A chocolate groat with fluff on it*
- *A 'one child gets in free' voucher to see the lunatics at Bedlam*
- *An apple core*

---

19 This is as a result of the embarrassment of the situation, not because the Pirate Captain is too bright and shiny for the albino pirate's sensitive eyes.

'Oh . . .' The Captain pushed the contents about with his fork. 'Is that it?'

'Those foreign coins could be valuable,' said the pirate in green hopefully.

'This one's from Water-flumeland,' said the Pirate Captain, holding it up to the light, 'which I don't think is even a real country.'

'We tried our best!' said the pirate with rickets, distraught.

'I know you did,' said the Pirate Captain. 'And I'm touched, really I am. But we're in a pickle. We've tried treasure maps and showbusiness, and you've already said you don't much care for me pulling the gold teeth from every man here. So if you know any other way a pirate can come by a bit of loot, I'd certainly like to hear it.'

'Why don't you become the spokesperson for treasure?' said the sassy pirate. 'My uncle was the spokesperson for Beecham's Pills, and he got a lifetime's supply of them for free. You should do that, but for gold and jewels and that kind of thing – I'm sure they'd like to be associated with you.'

'Or we could start making shell animals, to sell as souvenirs. Everybody likes shell animals, and we have ready access to plenty of shells.'

'Or we could,' said the pirate in red, rolling his eyes, 'try some pirating.'

'Eh?'

'You know – attacking boats and making off with

their treasure. What with us being pirates and all.'

Even though the Pirate Captain didn't care much for the pirate in red's tone, he had to admit that the idea had a certain logic. Now the pirate in red had pointed it out, the Pirate Captain wasn't really sure why it hadn't occurred to them earlier. So after they had finished their breakfast and drunk some coffee, the noisy pirate climbed up to the crow's nest[20] to look out for passing boats to plunder, whilst the rest of the crew got busy, polishing the cannons and swabbing the decks. They hoisted the Jolly Roger, to show they were back in business, but some of the younger pirates felt the skeleton face was a little too frightening, so they took it back down and used a flag that showed the Pirate Captain waving instead. The Pirate Captain himself took up his position at the ship's wheel and rested his hat on a barrel in order to let his glossy hair and beard billow in the wind. He was just thinking how he might get a portrait commissioned in exactly this pose when they spotted their first boat.

Pirating being a lot like riding a bicycle or making out with a pretty girl, the basics soon came back to them. They braced the mainsail and fired the cannons and fixed their faces into terrible grimaces, did all the usual roaring and generally made for a fairly horrific

---

20 Early sailors used actual crows to help with navigation, which were kept in cages at the top of the main mast. A released crow would inevitably head for land, allowing the ship's navigator to plot a course. If it didn't find land, the crow presumably just fell into the sea and died.

sight.[21] The pirates were slightly disappointed that the boat turned out to be a leper ship. The lepers were really very understanding, and the pirates came away with some nice bells and a hefty stack of old leper parts, which they thought they might be able to sell to hospitals later on. [22] The second boat they attacked was full of children out on a school trip. The pirates made a few doubloons by selling the children some opium, and they all had a great time together building Frankensteins out of the bits of leper they had just collected. When it was time to go home several of the children asked if they could maybe stay and be pirates too, but the Pirate Captain was adamant that they should get back to their mothers, who would be worrying about where they were.

The pirate with a scarf picked up a telescope – making sure to check the eyepiece first, because on board the pirate boat the general consensus seemed to be that 'the old gags were the best' – and scanned the horizon.

'Ship ahoy, Captain.'

'Well, third time lucky,' said the Pirate Captain, a little

---

21 When he wasn't inventing games, Blackbeard used to have hemp wicks coated with saltpetre attached to his hat, which when lit would envelop his face in a cloud of smoke to make himself look demonic. He was also famed for belching loudly to intimidate his victims.

22 There are two forms of leprosy, tuberculoid (dry) and lepromatous (wet). The former is characterised by death of nerves and is less contagious. In advanced cases, the latter can result in leontiasis which makes the victim's face look like a lion.

wearily. 'It's definitely not penniless refugees or a ghost ship or something like that?'

'Can't quite tell, Captain. Bit small. Well weathered, but somehow ... I don't know ... almost *noble*. And she's covered with ivory, by the looks of it.'

'That sounds more like it. Ivory. White gold! Remember our adventure with elephants?'

'Does it have a name?' said Jennifer, biting excitedly on a cutlass blade.

'The *Pequod*,'

'Funny sort of name for a boat.'

'Pirate Captain!' cried the albino pirate, and he came hurrying up, all out of breath and anxious-looking. 'We haven't got any cannonballs! We used them all up on the lepers and the school kids.'

'Honestly!' roared the Pirate Captain, 'what sort of an outfit are we running here? How can we not have any cannonballs?'[23]

'Well, we haven't got much of anything.'

---

23 Cannons of the time required round iron cannonballs. It was important to store the cannonballs so that they could be of instant use when needed, yet not roll around the gun deck. The solution was to stack them up in a square-based pyramid next to the cannon. The top level of the stack had one ball, the next level down had four, the next had nine, the next had sixteen, and so on. The only real problem was how to keep the bottom level from sliding out from under the weight of the higher levels. To do this, they devised a small brass plate ('brass monkey') with one rounded indentation for each cannonball in the bottom layer. Brass was used because the cannonballs wouldn't rust to it as they would to an iron one. When temperature falls, brass contracts in size faster than iron. So as it got cold on the gun decks, the indentations in the brass monkey would get smaller than the iron cannonballs they were holding. If the temperature got cold enough, the bottom layer would pop out of the indentations, spilling the entire pyramid over the deck. Hence the expression 'cold enough to freeze the balls off a brass monkey'.

The Pirate Captain had the scarf-wearing pirate bring up the inventory to conduct a quick recap:

> *20 limes*
> *1 Prize Ham*
> *2 dry cured hams*
> *3 barrels of tar*
> *1 pirate with an accordion (deceased and*
> *subsequently electroplated)*

'We've finished all the biscuits?' asked the Captain in dismay.

'I'm afraid so, Captain.'

'We could fire a lime, sir,' suggested the pirate with a scarf. 'They're sort of the right shape.'

'Aaaarrr. Fair enough,' said the Pirate Captain. 'But dip it in tar so they think it's a cannonball. Otherwise we risk looking stupid.'

'Can we wear those dinosaur masks we picked up at the Natural History Museum on our last adventure?' asked the pirate who was always getting nosebleeds. 'I really think they add to our ferociousness.'

'Why not?' roared the Pirate Captain. 'You know I'm always encouraging you lot to improvise. Express yourselves! Above all else remember that it's meant to be fun – that's the secret of good pirating.'

So the pirates fired the *Lovely Emma*'s cannons a couple of times and drew up alongside the *Pequod*. The

Pirate Captain grabbed hold of a hefty rope, swung across to the other boat – showing considerable athleticism, and not a little leg – and landed square in the middle of its deck. One of the *Pequod*'s men charged forward waving a dangerous-looking harpoon, but the Pirate Captain hacked at him with his cutlass and the man dropped to the deck, split right down the middle. Seeing this grisly spectacle, the rest of the *Pequod*'s crew backed off a bit, and the Pirate Captain was left face to face with a single brave soul.

'I'm the Pirate Captain!' said the Pirate Captain, twirling his cutlass like a baton in a move he had been up practising all the previous night. 'And I'm here for the loot!'

The man made no reply, but somehow his silence was fearsome in itself. A horrible sense of familiarity settled over the Pirate Captain. He squinted again at the fellow, and at his mop of straggly grey hair, and at the ugly scar that ran the length of one of his cheeks, and at the ivory leg poking out from the bottom of his trousers, and began to realise the terrible awkwardness of his situation.

'Oh dear,' said the Pirate Captain, turning a bright red.

Eight

DAMN YOU I SAY, DR. CHESINGTON!

In piratical circles this sort of thing was social death. For a moment the Pirate Captain thought about trying to pretend that he and the crew were some sort of pirate-a-gram, sent by one of Ahab's whaler mates. But whalers were a notoriously humourless lot, and it didn't seem likely they would have instigated such a thing.

'How incredibly embarrassing,' stuttered the Captain, grinning a weak grin. 'What are the odds? I mean, all the traffic cluttering up the shipping lanes nowadays, and I should run into you . . .'

The Pirate Captain trailed off. Ahab still hadn't said anything, but he seemed ready to explode. An angry-looking nerve had started to twitch in the corner of his eye. The Pirate Captain looked at his shoes. 'Sorry about running through, erm . . .'

'Mister Starbuck,' said Ahab icily.

'Yes. Sorry about running Mister Starbuck through. Do you think he'll be okay?'

'You've cleaved him clean in two.'

'I sort of have, haven't I? I bet I couldn't manage that again if I tried a thousand times! I – uh – hope that cannonball didn't do too much damage.'

'It wasn't a cannonball. It was a lime.'

'Yes. Well. Sorry anyway.'

'I have citric acid in my eye.'

'Oh. That must sting.'

'It does.'

The Pirate Captain awkwardly put away his cutlass, and waved for his pirate crew to stop their pirating. It was always nice to run into old acquaintances again, but this did pretty much scupper the whole operation. After all, there was a certain set of piratical ethics to be adhered to, and not stealing from a man who had offered you grog was just about at the top of the list.[24]

To try and make amends, the Pirate Captain invited Ahab and his crew to a meal on board the *Lovely Emma*. Usually the Pirate Captain wasn't much for having people to dinner, because it just meant less food for the pirates, but it seemed the least he could do, and he was

---

24 Pirates were not entirely amoral. The otherwise bloodthirsty Bartholemew Roberts couldn't bring himself to kill a priest, even when he refused to become the pirate's chaplain. So he let the man go, but only after stealing two prayer books and a corkscrew from him.

actually quite pleased he had a guest to show off the new boat to.

'I like your *Pequod*,' said the Pirate Captain. 'Especially what you've done with all that whalebone about the place. I'm afraid that I'm not as creative as yourself, so all the fittings on board the *Lovely Emma* are just solid silver. I think the sails are made from chinchilla skin. And the ropes are all woven from the hair of only the best-looking women actresses.'

'She seems a sturdy vessel, Pirate Captain,' agreed Ahab grudgingly.

'We even have a dance studio. I only found that yesterday. Does the *Pequod* have a dance studio on board?'

'No, Pirate Captain, it does not. I do not approve of dance.'

'That's a pity. How about cup holders? Does the *Pequod* have any cup holders? Because the *Lovely Emma* has them all over the shop. No need to ever spill a drop of grog.'

'I do not approve of grog on board ship, Pirate Captain.'

'Aaarrrr,' said the Pirate Captain, who was beginning to think that Ahab wasn't turning out to be the best dinner guest in the world. 'I hope you haven't got anything against chops?' he added, as a big pile of chops was carried to the table by a couple of the pirate crew. The pirates and the whalers started to eat in awkward silence.

'So, Ahab,' said the Pirate Captain, trying to get the conversation going. 'Any luck finding that whale?'

Ahab's stony face seemed to set even harder.

'No, Pirate Captain. The beast has continued to evade me these past few days. Just last night I thought I'd finally cornered him, but it turned out to be a big bit of kelp.'

'I'm sure it's an easy mistake to make,' said the Pirate Captain sympathetically. 'It sounds a lot like the time I got into all that confusion with a mermaid.'

'A mermaid?' repeated Ahab, actually raising an eyebrow, though the rest of his face remained as impassive as ever.

'Oh yes. I went out with this charming mermaid for ... oooh, how long would you say it was, Number Two?'

'About three months, Captain,' said the pirate with a scarf, looking a little pained.

'Yes, about three months. It took that long for the lads to convince me that it wasn't really a mermaid at all. It was just a regular fish.'

'Surely,' said Ahab, 'it is an easy enough distinction to make?'

'You would have thought that,' agreed the Captain, 'but what you have to appreciate is that the top half of that fish was just really very attractive. Normally I prefer the top halves of ladies to have arms and hair and all that, but this girl – or marlin, as I later came to realise – really carried it off. And she was a fantastic kisser.'

Ahab looked unimpressed. The Pirate Captain wondered if he should bring up the time they had sailed through an electrical storm and he had become magnetised, but somehow he felt Ahab wouldn't approve of that either.

'So, tell us all about whales then, Ahab,' said Jennifer eagerly.

'They're disgusting creatures,' said Ahab. 'Entirely without redeeming qualities.'

'But valuable, eh? You must make a packet from hunting them?'

'No, young lady. They're worthless. The "vermin of the sea". That's what I call them. And the white whale is the worst of the lot.'

'So why do you bother with them?'

'I hate them. I hate their small eyes, and I hate their wide mouths,' said Ahab, getting so annoyed his knuckles began to turn white.

'I'm a lot like that with mimes,' said the Captain with a nod. 'Can't bear them. All that pretending to get out of invisible boxes. Nonsense.'

'Whales are worse,' snarled Ahab. He viciously speared a piece of meat and chewed it with grim determination.

The other pirates were doing their best to make conversation with the whaler crew, but they were a strange bunch, and most of their stories placed a lot more emphasis on icebergs and interminable months spent at sea rather than feasts and fighting. Also, just as one of the whalers would actually seem to be getting to the point of an anecdote, they were liable to wander off suddenly on long and rather dull tangents about whale anatomy or things like that. The pirate in red was more than a little relieved when his conversation with a funny-looking whaler with one tooth and a lot of tattoos was interrupted by the booming voice of the Captain.

'Oho! What's this?' said the Pirate Captain, fighting back a grin. 'I do believe . . . Oh my! Why if I'm not mistaken . . . it's the WHITE WHALE ITSELF!'

Ahab started out of his chair. Several of the whalers reached for their harpoons. Then through the door to the kitchen came the pirate with a scarf and the pirate with gout, carrying a huge plate on which there sat a great pile of mashed potato. The mashed potato had been moulded roughly into the shape of a whale. It had radishes for eyes. The whalers put down their harpoons and settled grumblingly back into their seats.

'Are you mocking me, sir?' asked Ahab with a steely stare.

'Goodness! No! Not at all,' said the Pirate Captain defensively. 'It's just – look, it's made from mashed potato.' He spooned a dollop of potato from the whale's flank. 'See? We thought it would be a nice surprise,' he added sadly.

Ahab exhaled. 'I apologise. The truth is I'm tired, Pirate Captain. Tired of the ocean, and of this chase. In fact, we were heading back to Nantucket when you attacked.'

'Oh dear,' said the Pirate Captain. 'You mean to say you've given up? You're just going to let that whale mess about in the sea, splashing around and biting bits off of people?'

Ahab stood up and tapped the table with his whale-bone foot until he had everybody's attention. His baleful eyes swept the room and seemed to look deep into the souls of every man there.

'Hold!' he shouted. 'Before you stands Ahab, a man. For the past age I have abandoned my humanity in pursuit of the demon that ate my leg. I have stared at raging seas, through storm and rain, until moss grew upon my clothes and icicles hung from my ears and nose. Aye! I have not relented. The bulldog which grips on until death – that has been Ahab. The sun which beats on the desert without reprieve – that has been Ahab. The stubborn stain which soap will not shift – that has been Ahab. The Vale of Death holds no horrors for me, for I seek only vengeance, which I shall pursue even after I lie beneath the mould of the grave.'

The Pirate Captain was about to suggest that perhaps Ahab might want to think about developing some other hobbies outside whaling, but the old whaler had not quite finished.

'My destiny is fixed – I shall be avenged. But of late I have grown weary and my stomach queasy when we hit choppy waters. Also, this is my last spare whalebone leg and if he snaps this one, Ahab is stuffed. So!' Ahab paused and did his looking-into-souls-with-his-eyes trick again. 'I have decided to put a price on the whale's accursed head and return to Nantucket.'

The whalers gasped and not a few of them looked absolutely delighted. Ahab produced a sheaf of leaflets which he handed to the Pirate Captain.

'Take one and pass them on, Captain. And read it – read it well. For I offer a reward of six thousand doubloons to the man who brings me the white whale.'

The pirates looked at the leaflets, which showed the details of the reward above a picture of a whale chomping on a leg.

'SIX THOUSAND DOUBLOONS!' shouted Ahab, to emphasise the point. Then he sat down and tucked into his fruit medley.

'That's a big reward,' remarked the Pirate Captain, 'for catching a fish.'

Ahab shrugged. 'I told you. I really, *really* don't get on with him.'

Nine

I RIDE WITH THE BANDIT KING!

After a game of chess that the Pirate Captain later told the pirates he deliberately let Ahab win because he still felt guilty about Mister Starbuck, they waved the crew of the *Pequod* goodbye. The Captain ordered all the pirates into one of the *Lovely Emma*'s spacious meeting rooms, where they sat trying to look studious as he wrote some things down on a blackboard. It wasn't easy, because keeping quiet and sitting still were not traits at which pirates tended to excel. The Pirate Captain wrote down TREASURE HUNTING in capital letters and then he crossed it through. Then he wrote SHOWBUSINESS and he crossed that out too, but with a bit more venom this time so that the chalk snapped off and hit the octagon-faced pirate in the eye.

After that he wrote ACTUAL PIRATING and he crossed that out as well. Finally he wrote down WHALING and instead of crossing it out he drew a little tick and a smiley face next to it.

'I hope that makes everything clear,' said the Pirate Captain.

The crew muttered to each other, and the pirate in red put his hand up.

'I'm not saying it isn't a good idea, Pirate Captain,' he said. 'But you haven't really explained how we actually do it. The whaling, that is.'

'Oh, you know. Track the whale down, and bop him on the head.'

'Bop him on the head?'

The Pirate Captain mimed bopping the whale on the head. 'Bop. That's right. Something like that.'

'But how do we *find* the whale?' persisted the pirate in red, folding his arms and frowning to convey as much surliness as he dared.

The Pirate Captain looked stumped. His experience of this kind of thing was pretty limited. He had won a sizeable goldfish on Brighton Pier once, but that had involved throwing brightly coloured balls at coconuts, and he didn't really think that would do the trick in this case.

'Aarrr,' he said, drawing a few wavy lines on the blackboard and trying to sound knowledgeable. 'It's basically just a question of luring the whale onto your boat.'

'With magnets?' asked the sassy pirate.

'No. Not with magnets. I know you lot tend to think everything can be solved with magnets, but that's just not the case.'[25]

'What then?'

'Bait. We need to put out some whale bait.'

He wrote 'BAIT' on the blackboard and tapped it with his cutlass.

'What do we use for whale bait?' said the pirate with a hook for a hand.

'Whatever it is that whales like to eat.'

'Ooh! I know this!' said the pirate in green, waving his hand in the air. 'The answer's plankton. P-L-A-N-K-T-O-N.'

'You useless lubber!' roared the Pirate Captain. 'That's what they get to eat all the time. We need something that whales like *better* than plankton.'

'Ham?' suggested the pirate with rickets.

The Pirate Captain ran a hand through his luxuriant beard. He couldn't imagine a single creature, marine or otherwise, that wouldn't like ham. But they only had two regular hams left, and he didn't think he could bear to be parted from either of them. And he would sooner cut off his own stentorian nose than dangle his prize ham into the sea, only for some sea-beast to slobber all over it.

---

25 In fact, it is suspected that whales use the magnetic field of the Earth for navigation during their long migrations across the oceans. Many mass whale beachings occur at places where there is in an anomaly in the Earth's magnetic field.

'You have to remember that this is no ordinary whale,' he said authoritatively. 'It's a white whale. And whales aren't normally white, are they? So it makes sense to suppose that it turned white by eating albinos. We'll start off by dangling the albino pirate over the side of the boat for a few days.'

The albino pirate seemed a little nonplussed by this idea. The other pirates cheered and slapped him on the back.

'I don't know what the rest of you are looking so smug about,' said the Pirate Captain. 'Just in case my albino theory is wrong – because believe it or not, I am wrong very occasionally – I want to see you lot swimming behind the boat, disguised as krill. Gigantic, fat, delicious krill.[26] That's sure to whet his appetite.'

The crew let out a collective groan that the Captain cut dead with his best withering look.

'Pirate Captain?' the pirate in red asked again. 'Is it really necessary for your plans to always involve us dressing up as something? Because some might say it borders on an unhealthy obsession.'

'Last time I checked, krill are tiny bioluminescent shrimp-like organisms that don't give backchat,' said the Pirate Captain with a sniff and a glower.

'Will *you* be dressing up as whale bait, Captain?'

---

26 *Meganyctiphanes norvegica* form the base of many food chains around the world. Krill migrate daily, spending the daylight hours in deep waters and coming to the surface to feed and lay eggs at night.

'Obviously I'd love to,' said the Pirate Captain, rubbing the blackboard clean. 'But all that briny water could play havoc with my luxuriant beard. I'd hate to upset our large gay following, specifically those whose term for a hirsute gentleman such as myself is "a bear". Can't mess with the power of the pink pound! And it would be a shame not to share a nomenclature with such a fine animal.'

Some of the pirates looked unconvinced by the Pirate Captain's logic.

'There is also a chance we get our pirating powers from my beard, like Samson did in that book. So there's another reason why I can't help.'

'Try to look more tasty!' the pirate with long legs shouted to the albino pirate.

The albino pirate's head resurfaced and he spat out a mouthful of seawater. 'I don't think this is really working. I've been nibbled by crabs and licked by a shark, but there's no sign of any whales!'

'You've only been in there an hour,' said the pirate in green.

'I can't feel my arms or legs!'

'How's it going, Number Two?' said the Pirate Captain, relaxing in the *Lovely Emma*'s deck-side paddling pool. He was reading a book about whales.

'We lost another cabin boy,' said the scarf-wearing pirate.

'Not the funny little one with the old man's face?' said the Pirate Captain, almost dropping his book.

'I'm afraid so, Pirate Captain. A barracuda ate him.'

'Good grief! Poor cabin boy. So young!'

'But with an old man's face,' said the pirate with a scarf wistfully.

'Yes. That's what gave him such character. Our adventures won't be the same without him.'

'And we've also lost quite a few krill-pirates to sharks and drowning,' added the pirate with a scarf.

'A funny thing about that,' said the Pirate Captain, nodding at his book about whales. 'It turns out that my research might not have been quite up to scratch. Apparently sperm whales don't eat krill at all. They're actually quite fussy eaters. Around eighty per cent of their diet is squids.'

This caused some grumbling from a few of the bedraggled krill-pirates swimming behind the boat. The Captain waved and shot them a guilty grin.

'Not to worry, lads. That isn't the only thing I've learnt. This is why I'm always trying to encourage you lot to read more, because you can discover some fascinating things from books. It says here that whales, despite their brutish appearance, are in fact famed for being the most sensitive and romantic creatures in the animal kingdom, not only tending to mate for life but also able to communicate with each other over distances of thousands of miles.'

'That's sweet, Captain, but I'm not sure I see how it helps us,' said the scarf-wearing pirate.

The Pirate Captain looked serious. 'It so happens, Number Two, that a love of the theatre has not been the only outlet for the more poetic aspects of my soul. You know all those times I've disappeared into my cabin and not allowed anybody to disturb me? It will come as a shock for you to learn that I've not really been studying my nautical almanacs as I may have previously led you to believe.'

'To be honest, Captain,' said the pirate in red, 'we always suspected that you might have been looking at that book of saucy etchings you keep on the top of your wardrobe.'

'Well I've not been doing that either, not that I have a clue what you're talking about. The fact is, these past few months I have been writing a *novel*. It's a romance.'

And somewhat sheepishly the Captain produced a manuscript from under his hat.

'I'm aware that this kind of thing is slightly frowned upon by the pirating fraternity, so obviously I will be using a pen-name, should the frankly narrow-minded publishing industry ever choose to recognise my talents.'

The pirate crew breathed a quiet sigh of relief, because they could imagine what the Pirate King would have to say if he ever got wind of this.

'So what's the plan, Captain?'

'We'll simply do that trick of tying a couple of tin cans together with a piece of string,' explained the Pirate Captain, 'and then dangle one of the cans into the ocean so that the white whale is able to hear me read my novel aloud. Obviously I will do different voices for the various characters. It will be a lot like that business with Theseus and those Sirens – because of his sensitive soul the white whale will find himself drawn irresistibly towards us, and just as he's finding his huge baleen heart touched to the very core by my meditations on love and fate, bang! We harpoon him through the brain.'

The pirates almost all agreed that this sounded like a pretty foolproof plan.

'I'm very impressed, Captain,' said the pirate with a scarf. 'I didn't think you had it in you to write an entire novel. It's quite an achievement.'

'Oh, well, it's only about thirty-one thousand words,' said the Pirate Captain modestly. 'Bit cheeky to call it a novel really.'

The pirates fixed up the cans and string and then gathered around as the Pirate Captain made himself comfortable on a barrel. He cricked his neck and cleared his throat.

'*The Pirate Of My Heart,*' he began to read. 'Chapter One: "Love Across a Moonlit Sea".'

'Emerald was a proud, independent woman, fiery red locks of hair tumbling about her alabaster shoulders. She was free from that arrogant buccaneer, and she knew that fact should bring her only joy. But she could not help but think of his last words to her, those mischievous glittering eyes, and that firm, magnificent beard.

' "Emerald," he had said, "you are a treasure! Just like a real emerald! But you are an Irish princess, and I am a Pirate Captain! One day I shall make you mine, but for now I must go, and plunder the Spanish Main ..."

'... Emerald looked under her pillow, and there she found a single white rose, as well as a battered old eye-patch. So perhaps it hadn't been a dream after all.'

The Pirate Captain closed his book and all the pirates clapped. But even though Emerald had made the right decision to follow her feelings and not marry the swarthy Spanish Duke, there was still no sign of the whale.

'Not to worry, Pirate Captain,' said the pirate in green. 'It must be that whales are not so clever and sensitive as people make out. Because your story was very good.'

'Yes,' agreed the pirate with long legs. 'I especially liked the way Emerald learned that the best way to get somebody to like you is simply to be yourself. Though of course it helps when yourself is a beautiful princess.'

'You enjoyed it then?' asked the Pirate Captain. 'Be honest though, because I really do value your opinions.'

The pirate in red looked as if he was about to say something, but the Captain hadn't quite finished. 'When I say "honest opinion" I'd like you to bear two things in mind. One – I don't take criticism particularly well at all, even the constructive kind. And two – I'm the Captain of this boat and I have an extremely sharp cutlass.'

The pirates' next plan was slightly less sensitive. 'I once saw a man doing this in the Thames,' explained the Pirate Captain with a wink to his second-in-command, as a couple of the pirates rolled a barrel of gunpowder off the side of the boat into the sea.

There was a muffled explosion, and then a few dead fish floated up to the surface. The Pirate Captain looked a little put out. 'But seeing as this is the ocean, which is a little bigger than the Thames, we might need a bit more gunpowder. Fetch us another couple of barrels, Number Two.'

A plume of water splashed across the deck and a shower of fish and lobsters crashed down onto the pirates' heads. The pirates looked about hopefully, but all they could see was a dying shark draped over the yardarm looking disappointedly back at them. 'No whales there,' said the pirate with a hook for a hand. They rolled a few more barrels off the side of the boat. Another huge wave crashed over the pirates, drenching them from head to toe, and another burst of creatures and seaweed rained onto the deck. The pirates prodded about in the mess.

'Still can't see him,' said the pirate in green, a bit of tentacle wriggling limply on his hat.

Jennifer pulled a starfish out of her top. 'It's fun though, isn't it?'

After the pirates ran out of barrels of gunpowder, the Pirate Captain had the bright idea of emptying all the *Lovely Emma*'s lamps and pouring the oil out from the back of the boat, because he remembered reading somewhere that oil slicks were a great way of catching sea-creatures. But all they ended up with were a few rather sad-looking seagulls. The pirates felt a little guilty and scooped them up in big nets to give them a clean. The oil didn't come off very well even with lots of scrubbing, so the pirate in red suggested that the oily seagulls might make quite good candles instead. Everybody agreed that this was a good idea, because they had run out of lamp oil.

There was an almighty 'pop' and the pirate with a cauli-flower ear disintegrated in an explosion of fireworks. The other pirates 'oohed' and 'aahed' as roman candles and rockets zoomed off into the sky. The pirate with a scarf crossed another item off his clipboard.

'How many schemes is that?' asked the Pirate Captain.

'Fifteen schemes,' said the pirate with a scarf. 'Sixteen if you include the business with the pig.'

'Aaarrr. Best forget that one.'

'It's not going too well, is it, Pirate Captain?' said the scarf-wearing pirate, staring at the conspicuously whale-less sea. 'I'm worried that perhaps this whaling busi-ness is a little more difficult than we thought. Possibly that's why Ahab said he'd been chasing the whale for years.'

'Pish,' said the Pirate Captain, trying to sound upbeat. 'What you have to remember is that Ahab never had my maverick sideways approach to problem-solving. It's all in hand.'

He waved that morning's post at the scarf-wearing pirate and started to flick through it.

'Bill, bill, bill, cutlass catalogue, bill ... Ah-ha! Here we go.' He held up one of the letters triumphantly. 'This'll sort us out, Number Two! I took the precaution of writing to our old friend Scurvy Jake. You know what an outdoors type he is. He even took a job in Brighton Sea Life Centre for a bit whilst he was working his way through pirate academy. So he's bound to know a thing or two about catching fishes! Let's see now ... "Dear Pirate Captain",' read the Pirate Captain. ' "Thanks for the letter. It's great to hear from you after our last adventure with the monkey wrestling. Since then I've been ... blah ... new job as a grill chef ... blah blah ... remember the old days ... blah blah blah ... might get a new hat ... blah blah blah blah ... the most beautiful sunset you can imagine" – good grief, man! Get to the point! Ah, here we are: "About the whale. Interesting question ... Have you tried dangling that albino chap over the side? Failing that, try magnets! Lots of love, Scurvy Jake".'

The Pirate Captain sighed, and muttered a terrible nautical oath under his breath. He noticed that another of the envelopes had a Nantucket postmark and felt a sudden nasty queasiness deep in his belly. He considered hiding the letter under the astrolabe in his office without reading it, because that was the Pirate Captain's usual way of dealing with letters that he thought might contain bad news, but against his better judgement he opened it up. His salty face turned ashen.

'Is everything okay, Pirate Captain?' asked the scarf-wearing pirate anxiously.

'Aaarrr. Nothing to worry about. It's just a friendly reminder from Cutlass Liz,' said the Pirate Captain, attempting to shoot him a reassuring smile, but finding his mouth stuck in a sort of lop-sided grimace. 'Look here, she's even included a helpful illustration.'

The scarf-wearing pirate looked at the picture on the letterhead, which showed Cutlass Liz merrily dismembering a pirate. There was a speech bubble coming from the pirate's mouth. It said:

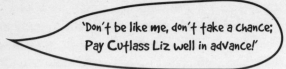

'Don't be like me, don't take a chance;
Pay Cutlass Liz well in advance!'

The Pirate Captain took a few deep breaths and tried to concentrate on calm things, like lapping waves and pan-pipes. But the vein in his temple was starting to throb, and he could feel a steady panic rising from the soles of his pirate boots.

'I seem to be getting one of my heads,' said the Pirate Captain. And with that he walked very slowly below decks, pausing only briefly to screw Scurvy Jake's letter into a ball and throw it at a passing seagull.

Ten

SWIMMING POOLS
OF PASSION!

The pirates lay miserably in their bunks. It had been the best part of a fortnight since they had decided to take up whaling, and they still hadn't seen so much as a blowhole. For the first few days the Pirate Captain had simply glowered and stomped about a bit more than he usually did. But just recently he had started to behave in a more and more alarming fashion. He would spend the nights stalking the deck, muttering darkly to himself, and the days refusing to come out of his cabin. He had taken to bellowing bleak self-penned poetry through the *Lovely Emma*'s speaking tubes. And he hadn't so much as brushed his beard in days. Right at that moment he was stood on the bow of the boat roaring and shaking his fist at the drizzling sky. Normally when the Pirate

Captain was in a mood he would have been secretly pleased that the weather reflected it, because the Pirate Captain's moods tended to just be for show. But this was an actual genuine mood, and he wasn't pleased at all.

'Oh dear. He's started shouting at the ocean again,' said the sassy pirate, listening to the faint bellowing sounds that filtered through the porthole.

'I think I prefer the shouting to all that relentless pacing about,' said the pirate in green.

'Or the poetry,' said the pirate with a peg-leg.

'Or the frowning,' said Jennifer.

'Did you see him this morning? I've never seen the vein in his temple get that big before.'

'He told me off for singing a shanty!'

'I took him some beef for dinner. But he wouldn't even let me in. It was specially larded and everything,' said the pirate with a scarf. [27]

'Larded?' said the sassy pirate, licking his lips.

'Yes, glistening with specks of visible fat. I tried wafting the smell under his door, but it was hopeless.'

'I thought I could cheer him up by riding up and down in the dumb waiter, but he just sat there with his arms folded.'

'No grog. No laughing. Lights out at seven p.m. This isn't what being a pirate is meant to be about at all!'

---

27 Larded beef (or any meat) has been artificially marbled with fat. Strips of suet or pork fat are run through the lean meat with a 'larding needle' to add extra moisture and flavour.

'We might as well be working in an *office*.'

'I hate whales!'

The pirates all jumped up as their bedroom door was thrown open with a crash.

'Up on deck, you swabs!' roared the Pirate Captain. A couple of the pirates had to fight back tears, because for once it really sounded like the Pirate Captain actually thought they were swabs, and wasn't just saying it to add some colourful nautical atmosphere. The crew all shuffled up the *Lovely Emma*'s spiral staircase and out on to the moonlit deck. The Pirate Captain hadn't even given the pirates time to put on their overcoats and so they had to strain to hear him over their chattering teeth. He pulled a big ham out from under his pirate coat. Not just any old ham, but the Captain's Prize Ham itself. The pirate crew gasped.

'Silence!' shouted the Pirate Captain, even though the pirates weren't saying anything. 'Do you see this ham?'

The pirates nodded.

'This is my prize honey-roast ham. Do you see?' he repeated. The pirates nodded again. The Pirate Captain rubbed it with his sleeve to bring up the shine on the glaze and advanced towards the mast with the ham held high.

'Whoever captures the whale, he shall have this ham!'

The Pirate Captain proceeded to nail the ham to the mast. Then he pulled an especially dour face and stormed back downstairs. The pirate crew were left on their own. They looked at each other in dismay.

'His Prize Ham!' said the albino pirate, wide-eyed.

'This is bad,' said the scarf-wearing pirate.

'I don't think I've ever even seen it out of its case before!' said the pirate with gout.

A mixture of emotions ran through the crew. One of the emotions was 'worry', because they realised that things must be pretty serious for the Pirate Captain to take such a drastic step as nailing his ham to the mast. And the other emotion was 'being really hungry', because with its delicious glaze gleaming in the moonlight, the ham looked like just about the loveliest thing any of them had ever seen. So they fetched some blankets to keep warm and sat in a big circle around the mast. Jennifer handed out notepaper to all the pirates so that they could write down their best whale-catching schemes. Some of the pirates rubbed their foreheads really hard to get their brains going, but all it did was make them feel dizzy.

The sun had come up and the pirates were still all sat around in a circle staring at their blank pieces of paper. They had drunk the *Lovely Emma*'s entire supply of coffee, but even that hadn't helped.

'How about something involving semaphore?' said the sassy pirate.

'Does anybody actually know semaphore?' said Jennifer.

Everybody went quiet again.

'It's no good,' said the scarf-wearing pirate, sticking out his lower lip and doodling a little picture of a sad manta ray. 'If the Captain can't come up with a way of catching the whale, then what chance have we got? None of us is as clever as the Captain.'

Even the pirate in red, who normally would have come out with some pithy and sarcastic comment, just nodded in agreement.

'What we need is help,' said Jennifer, 'from somebody just as smart as the Pirate Captain.'

The pirates looked at her dubiously.

'Somebody who's always got a plan. Somebody who is both cunning and ingenious.'

'No!' said the pirate with a scarf, suddenly catching her drift.

'Somebody with a beard that goes all the way up to his eyeballs,' said Jennifer.

'She can't mean!'

'She does!'

'The Pirate Captain will go mad!'

'He's already gone mad,' pointed out Jennifer. 'That's the whole problem.'

The pirates still looked unconvinced.

'I know it's a bit of a risk,' said Jennifer, 'but I for one can't spend another night listening to any more poems with titles like "The Screaming Face of Desolation".'

Eleven

BLOOD, BEER, AND A BUSTED BOAT!

The *Barbary Hen* lay anchored in a beautiful tropical bay that looked like something from a postcard or an expensive jigsaw puzzle. As the *Lovely Emma* pulled up alongside, the pirates could see some of Black Bellamy's crew playing on the beach and splashing about in the sea. The infamous captain seemed to have been recruiting, because there were a number of women in bikinis who the pirates didn't recognise from their previous encounters.

Black Bellamy himself was reclining in a hammock on the deck, drinking grog out of a coconut and talking to a blonde and a brunette. He must have been telling some pretty funny jokes, because the women were laughing at almost everything he said. Seeing the *Lovely Emma*, he waved languidly.

'Hello pirates!' he roared.

'Hello Black Bellamy!' shouted Jennifer. 'Could we have a word?'

'Dear lady! Of course, come aboard,' Black Bellamy shouted back. 'I may be the most diabolical pirate on the Seven Seas, but there's always a welcome on the *Barbary Hen* for a beautiful woman.'

The blonde and the brunette jumped up and placed a gangplank between the two boats, and then wandered off in a leggy way. Black Bellamy bounded from his hammock and helped Jennifer across. '*Enchanté,*' he said in French, kissing her hand.

'I hope we're not disturbing anything?' said Jennifer.

'Not at all, not at all. We're just taking a bit of shore leave after the Vegas run. Maxing and relaxing, that kind of thing,' said Black Bellamy, looking across at the *Lovely Emma*. 'It really is a nice boat you've got there, you know. Puts the *Barbary Hen* to shame. Tell me – was it the Pirate Captain's idea to put all those bits of squid in the rigging? And wrap that dead eel around the bow?'

'Um, sort of. Actually, Mister Bellamy, it's the Pirate Captain I need to talk to you about,' said Jennifer. 'He's gone a bit loopy.'

'Oh good grief! My poor old friend!' said Black Bellamy, putting his hand to his brow in horror. 'Well, we must discuss this properly. Over dinner. Come into my office and we'll talk all about it.'

Black Bellamy took Jennifer's hand and led her down-stairs to his office. He opened the door with a flourish and waved her in. Nobody had held a door open for Jennifer since she'd left Victorian London.[28] She was very impressed. Black Bellamy had somehow managed to combine lavish ostentation with aesthetic restraint. The furniture was pretty classy stuff like chaise-longues and glass coffee tables, and Jennifer noticed several oil paintings that were of an even better quality than the ones in the Pirate Captain's office. There was Black Bellamy with his arm round the Emperor Ninko of Japan. And there he was with the eighteen-year-old Isabella II of Spain, holding up fish and fishing rods by a river – this one was signed 'With love to my main pirate, Izzi XXX'. There was a well-stocked trophy cabinet against one wall, with a couple of 'Beard Wearer of the Year' awards, and on the opposite wall he had a display case marked 'Rare Bird Eggs', full of dozens and dozens of peregrine falcon eggs. The whole room was suffused by the faint smell of seaweed.

Jennifer spotted a photograph of Black Bellamy's class from pirate academy sitting on his desk. She was surprised to see that even as a young pirate his beard went right up to his eyeballs. More surprising still was who was stood next to him. It was the Pirate Captain.

---

28 Gentlemen opening doors for Victorian ladies was not just a matter of manners. The big skirts and dresses of the day meant that a lady would be unable to get in and out of carriages and rooms unless someone held the door open in advance.

His belly was perhaps a little less impressive, and he didn't have quite so many gold teeth, but it was definitely him.

'I didn't realise you'd known the Pirate Captain so long!' exclaimed Jennifer.

'Oh yes, we go way back,' said Black Bellamy, handing her a glass of rum. 'I think you'll find this a passable vintage. I'm told 1812 was a good year for grog.'

'So you were at school together?' asked Jennifer, her curiosity piqued.

'We were even roommates for a while. We were like *that*!' said Black Bellamy, crossing his fingers.

'But the Pirate Captain's always saying that you're his arch-nemesis and you don't miss an opportunity to mess him about, and that you're diabolical beyond measure,' said Jennifer.

'It's just banter, Jennifer. He's an old rogue!' replied Black Bellamy with a laugh.

Two of Black Bellamy's pirates brought in a selection of oysters and some other fancy shellfish.

'But enough about me,' said Black Bellamy, 'let's talk about you. How can I help *you*?'

'It's not me, Mister Bellamy ... it's the Captain. He's got himself all wound up about catching this whale. He's not himself.'

'Poor Pirate Captain. You've got really nice earrings, by the way. Nice and sparkly.'

'Thanks, that's very kind. So have you. But – uh – like

I was saying. The Pirate Captain. He's not even *eating* properly.'

'Yes, yes. Sorry to hear that – you're quite a distraction, you know,' said Black Bellamy.

'The thing is, we've tried to catch the whale to cheer him up, but we don't really know where to start. They're slippery creatures, these whales.'

'I can imagine. Now, you're a Gemini, aren't you?'

'Oh no, I'm a Leo.'

'I knew it! I can always tell. Your fiery lips give you away.'

'Really? You do say some things, Mister Bellamy.'

Black Bellamy leaned back in his chair, which served to show off his expansively hairy chest. He dabbed at his temple with a napkin. 'Is it just me, or is it rather hot in here?' he said.

'It is quite warm, yes.'

'Feel free to take a few of those layers off if you're uncomfortable.'

As the meal wore on, Jennifer began to think that Black Bellamy wasn't quite the villain she had been led to believe. He was certainly courteous, always leaning forward eagerly when she tried to reach a dish, or complimenting her on the way she held a fork. He was a good listener too, ever-ready with a compliment and extremely interested in her life and dress sizes. Admittedly, he was surprisingly clumsy – she lost count of the number of times he accidentally knocked the pepperpot to the floor and she had to bend over to pick it up. But really he wasn't such a bad sort at all.

'. . . and that's how I nursed that little kitten back to health,' said Black Bellamy at the end of a story. He cradled his hairy chin in his hand and looked thoughtfully into Jennifer's eyes.

'How wonderful,' said Jennifer, clapping. 'That's very similar to a story that the Pirate Captain tells about a kitten. Oh! The Pirate Captain! I'd almost forgotten why I was here!'

Black Bellamy muttered something under his breath.

'So can you help? Can you?'

Black Bellamy puffed out his cheeks. 'I'm very flattered you should ask. But what makes you think that I might succeed where such a clever young woman has failed? I'm just an unassuming pirate trying to make his way in the world like everybody else.'

'Oh no! Everybody knows how clever you are!'

'Oh *don't*! Really? What do they say?'

'The men are always saying how you're "confounded clever" and how your "cunning is surpassed only by the devil himself". Someone called you an evil genius!'

'I really can't believe that,' said Black Bellamy. Jennifer thought he was probably blushing underneath all that beard. 'Besides, I'd like to think I'm more of a "jovial nuisance" than an "evil genius". But this whale business – I'll see what I can do. When a lovely lady like yourself comes to ask, I can hardly refuse, can I?'

'Oh wow! Thanks Black Bellamy!' Jennifer leapt up and kissed him on the forehead. Then she held up her glass of grog. 'Let's drink to friendship!'

'Friendship! And ladies' faces!' roared Black Bellamy.

When Jennifer and Black Bellamy reappeared on the deck of the *Barbary Hen* they both waved at the pirates anxiously waiting on the *Lovely Emma*.

'He's going to help!' she said, hugging Black Bellamy. She ignored the immature pirates who went 'woooooo!' when they saw the hug.

'Thanks, Black Bellamy!' said the scarf-wearing pirate, helping Jennifer back across the plank. 'We won't forget this in a hurry!'

'It's nothing,' shouted Black Bellamy, as the *Barbary Hen* began to sail off. 'It's just so awful to hear that the Pirate Captain has gone a bit mental. When I think of his poor little mad face, I feel quite emotional.'

The pirates barely had time to get even halfway through an exciting game of Scrabble before the *Barbary Hen* sailed back into view. They all crowded around the boat's telescope and fought to see what was going on.

'He's back already!' said the albino pirate.

'He can't be!' said the pirate in red.

'He is! I don't believe it! And he's got the whale!' exclaimed the pirate with a scarf.

As the *Barbary Hen* came closer they could see Black Bellamy leaning nonchalantly on the ship's wheel, steering with one hand and examining the nails of his other. And there behind him, sat right in the middle of the deck, was a gigantic white whale strapped down by hefty nautical ropes. The whale flapped its tail and a steaming jet of spray erupted from its blowhole, catching the sunlight in a rainbow haze. It was an impressive-looking creature, thought the pirate with a scarf. He remembered how Charles Darwin, the young naturalist they had encountered on their previous adventure, had told him that if you got yourself twelve sets of pirate lungs and then stitched them all together, disgusting though it would be, they would still have just half the lung capacity of one of a whale's lungs. That wasn't the kind of statistic to be taken lightly.

'That Black Bellamy,' said the pirate with a hook for a hand. 'You've got to hand it to him, he's pretty good at stuff.'

Jennifer clapped her hands. 'Somebody go and get the Captain! He'll be over the moon!'

The pirate with a scarf ran down the stairs and came back a few moments later, followed by what the crew at first glance thought must be a dirty old tramp. The pirates all gasped when they realised that the shuffling, shabby mess wasn't a tramp – it was the Pirate Captain, wearing only a pair of grubby pyjama bottoms. His eyes were wild and staring, his face was anything but pleasant or open, and his beard was ratty and unmanageable. Blinking at the light, the Pirate Captain stared uncomprehendingly about. But as the *Barbary Hen* pulled up alongside the *Lovely Emma*, he spotted the whale and his mouth fell open.

'The white whale!' he croaked. Then he saw Black Bellamy. 'And you, you scoundrel!'

'Pirate Captain!' said Jennifer crossly. 'I'm so sorry, Mister Bellamy. He doesn't know what he's saying.' She turned back to the Pirate Captain. 'You're being very rude to Mister Bellamy.'

'No, no,' said Black Bellamy. 'It's quite understandable.' He looked sadly at his shoes. 'I know we've had our ups and downs, Pirate Captain. And I know that I've not been entirely honest with you in the past. But I'd just like you to think of this as a favour from an old friend. Your men told me that you were having a tough time of it and this seemed the least I could do.'

The Pirate Captain was really very touched. It was all he could do to try to stop his voice sounding too emotional. 'I don't know what to say,' he said.

'Then don't say anything at all, Pirate Captain,' said Black Bellamy, putting a finger to his lips. 'Except,' he added, 'there is just one small matter.' Black Bellamy paused. 'Obviously I went to the trouble of finding the whale for no more reward than to see my dear friend get back to his old self. But on my way here I happened to receive a heart-rending letter from some orphans. They need me to go and stop their orphanage being knocked down by greedy real-estate developers.'

'That's awful!' said the albino pirate.

'I know. I think of those orphans and I well up. I do,' said Black Bellamy, dabbing at the beard below his eyes. 'So, although I'd love to let you have the whale for nothing, I'd be grateful if you could just pay a nominal sum that I can then pass on to the orphans. To help them in their hour of need. I wouldn't even ask otherwise.'

'We haven't got much,' said the pirate with a scarf. 'Just the money we made from our Vegas show.'

Black Bellamy shrugged. 'Well, I'm sure those cripples will be very grateful for anything.'

'Cripples? I thought you said that they were orphans?' said Jennifer.

'Ah,' said Black Bellamy, 'orphan cripples, my dear. Terrible business. And some of them have the pox. Orphan cripple pox victims.'

The Pirate Captain felt so moved by Black Bellamy's devotion to the needy that he threw in the big stone coin and their few remaining limes as well. Black Bellamy grinned, pocketed the loot, and hopped back across to his boat.

'Make sure you feed him three times a day or he gets a bit restless,' he said as the crew of the *Barbary Hen* finished heaving the white whale onto the deck of the *Lovely Emma.* 'And above all else, whatever you do, *don't get him wet.* Whales hate getting wet, Pirate Captain.'

'But what about all that time they spend cavorting around in the ocean?' said the Pirate Captain. 'They love getting wet.'

'You'd think so, wouldn't you?' said Black Bellamy, laughing. 'But it's an old myth. They're mammals, remember? Just the same as you or me. Or a cow. And how many times have you seen a cow go for a swim?'

'I suppose you're right,' said the Pirate Captain. 'I'd never thought of it like that.'

And so the two sets of pirates said their goodbyes and set sail in different directions, Black Bellamy to help the orphan cripples and the Pirate Captain to Nantucket to collect Ahab's reward.

'That's a stroke of luck, eh lads?' said the Pirate Captain turning to the crew.

'Are you feeling better now, Captain?' asked the albino pirate.

'One of the advantages of having a temperament as unpredictable as mine is that you get over things like stress and depression extremely quickly.'

'Captain Ahab will be really pleased,' said the pirate with gout, giving the whale a pat.

'The only thing is, it's not as big as I was expecting,

Captain,' said the pirate in red, looking at the creature waggle its little flippers. 'I mean, Ahab made quite an issue about it being a leviathan. But it's really more a sort of middling-sized whale.'

'Aaarrr. He struck me as the type to exaggerate,' said the Pirate Captain breezily. 'Didn't he tell us that he'd combed every *inch* of the sea? That's obviously impossible – especially since Black Bellamy found him after twenty minutes! And besides, how many white whales could there possibly be knocking about?'

The pirates nodded.

'Now, I know I smell a bit ripe, so I'm off for a nice long soaky bath. You might want to air my duvets, Number Two.'

Twelve

I FOUGHT THE SARGASSO SQUID!

'Take that, pirate boat! Now I, the terrible sponge, am master of this ocean!'

The Pirate Captain was sat in the bath, and as always he was putting on a bit of a show whilst the scarf-wearing pirate scrubbed him clean. He made a sort of glugging noise and sank the sextant that was doubling as a pirate boat once and for all.

'It's a good job there aren't really gigantic sponge creatures about, isn't it?' he said, waggling the victorious sponge at his deputy. 'Or us pirates would be done for.'[29]

---

29 Sponges are amongst the simplest multicellular animals – loose collections of specialised cells combined to produce a more efficient feeding mechanism. They range from inconspicuous prickly layers growing on rocks to large, complex and beautiful structures such as Venus's flower-basket. None are capable of attacking a ship.

'You're right, sir. I often think just that.'

'But it's a shame the sea can't be full of lovely bubbles like this.'

'It *is* a shame,' agreed the pirate with a scarf sadly. His rugged brow was furrowed in concentration as he carefully soaped each delicate strand of the Pirate Captain's beard. He stood up and surveyed his handiwork.

'I think we can rinse her off now, Captain.'

'I hope she's going to be okay,' grimaced the Pirate Captain, gently supporting his soapy beard in his hands. 'Can't remember a time when I've let her get into such a mess.'

The pirate with a scarf reached across to turn on one of the big brass taps, but nothing came out. Not even a drop.

'That's not right,' said the scarf-wearing pirate. He tried to turn on the other tap, and nothing came out of that one either. The Pirate Captain looked horrified. He couldn't help but think back to their adventure in Tangiers when the water in the hotel at which the pirates were staying had given out and the Captain had been left in the same situation, completely unable to rinse out his beard except with seawater. Over the next couple of days it had puffed up into a ridiculous frizzy ball, and he had ended up looking more like one of those hats that Russian spy ladies wear than a respected old sea-dog.

So the Pirate Captain leapt from his tub and bounded onto the deck to try and find out what was amiss, naked as a new-born baby, except a good deal hairier and with a few more tattoos. For those readers who may be interested, the Pirate Captain's tattoos included:

- A map of an island across his belly. This had a big 'X' on it, which the Captain thought probably had something to do with treasure. Unfortunately, he had no idea where the island was, because like most of his tattoos, it was the product of an evening full of too much grog. He had just woken up in Portsmouth one morning and there it was.

- The Pirate King's face on his right bicep. He'd grown since it was done and now the tattoo was a bit misshapen, so that the Pirate King looked a little bit like he'd had a stroke.

- A picture of an anchor on his left forearm. This was to remind the Pirate Captain to drop anchor whenever they were leaving the boat. Otherwise it just tended to drift off, and the men would look at him accusingly.

- A shopping list on his shin, which had seemed like a good idea at the time.

- 'I've seen the lions at Longleat' on his left shoulderblade.

- 'Left' on his left foot and 'Right' on his right. A gift from his mother on his fourth birthday.

There the Pirate Captain stood, like a perfectly proportioned nude renaissance statue. He had always been extremely comfortable with his own naked body, but some of the pirate crew seemed quite overwhelmed by the sheer soapy spectacle. Looking about, hands on hips, it was instantly obvious to the Captain what the problem was. Somehow the wily whale had managed to slip from its moorings, and was now flopping about on the deck, causing all sorts of mischief. There were bits of broken barrel and squashed pirate everywhere. Most of the flower beds in the ornamental garden were ruined, and there was a big plume of water coming from where the whale had managed to bash a jagged hole in one of the *Lovely Emma*'s water pipes with a particularly vicious flick of its tail. The water that was meant for the Pirate Captain's beard was fountaining onto the deck, and raining down on the whale. The Captain watched in dismay as the creature began to change from a pearly white to a battleship grey. A great big puddle of paint collected around the base of the whale and seeped towards the Pirate Captain's toes.

'Don't get it wet,' he muttered to himself. 'That Black Bellamy. He's ... he's ...'

'The living end?' suggested the pirate in red.

'Exactly.' The Pirate Captain made a mental note to get a new tattoo that said something terrible about Black Bellamy's mother.

'He didn't find the white whale at all! We've been

duped! The cove probably just stole this regular whale from the nearest zoo!'

The Pirate Captain paced around the creature. 'Well, lads,' he said. 'We'll just have to slap on some more paint and hope that Ahab doesn't look at the thing too closely. You and you,' he pointed at the pirate in red and the new pirate with an accordion, 'Come on, you cozening brace of dandies! You're on whale-painting detail.'

None of the pirates was particularly good at plumbing, so the Captain had to finish washing his beard off in the spray of water bursting from the broken pipe. Then he went downstairs and, after getting dressed, spending a few minutes tying ribbons in his beard and practising some victorious faces for the benefit of Cutlass Liz, the Pirate Captain strode back onto the deck to see how the whale painting was going. He was glad to see that they'd managed to paint about half of the beast's great face a nice shade of 'Orchid Haze'. The effect was only spoilt by the elegantly curled moustache and big bushy eyebrows that the whale was now sporting. The Pirate Captain had a pretty good idea as to whose handiwork this was.

'You!' he said, pointing at the pirate in red. 'What are you playing at?'

The pirate in red sidled guiltily along a flipper.

'I just thought it gave him a bit of character,' he said. 'I was going to paint a little top hat as well. To make him a gentleman whale.'

'I'll paint you a new *@#*&!' roared the Pirate Captain. It wasn't often that he used language, but the pirate in red had been riding his luck for the whole adventure.

'You're always saying we should express ourselves creatively,' whined the pirate in red.

'Scrub it off! Right now, you cove!'

The Pirate Captain folded his arms and contemplated the whale. He looked across at his trusty deputy.

'What do you think, Number Two?' said the Pirate Captain. 'Not quite there, is it?'

'Hard to say, Captain,' said the pirate with a scarf.

'I mean – Ahab may be a monomaniacal old bore, but he doesn't look like he'd be easily cheated.' The Pirate Captain's eyebrows drooped a bit.

'No, sir. He's a bit of a stickler for detail, I'd say.'

The two pirates fell into a thoughtful silence and stared at the shiny white whale. Then a wily look crept over the Pirate Captain's face.

'You know what would help, Number Two?'

'What's that, Captain?'

'If this whale were to *confess* to being the whale who ate Ahab's leg.'

The pirate with a scarf pulled a bit of a face, and not for the first time wondered if his Captain might not have been spending a bit too much time under tropical suns of late.

'No, hear me out,' said the Pirate Captain, catching his look. 'Do you remember the story of Jonah?'

'Not really, sir.'

'Well, the gist of the thing is that back in biblical times a man goes to live inside a whale for a bit. I forget the exact reason, probably to avoid having to make boat repayments. Not much of a story, but that's the Bible for you.'

'Are you going anywhere with this, Captain?'

'All it needs is for one of us pirates to hide inside the belly of the whale. That way if old Ahab raises any doubts about the veracity of our catch, the swallowed pirate can loudly proclaim how he's the very same whale that ate his leg off. To the outside world it will seem that it's the whale doing the talking, especially if we devise some kind of apparatus to move the whale's mouth up and down while the pirate speaks. Lip-synching the thing will be the key. If you can call it lip-synching, seeing as I don't think whales can be described as having any lips to speak of.'

There was a bit of an argument between the pirates as to whether whales had lips *per se*, with the conclusion being that whilst they had definite edges to their mouths, they were more like gums than lips. A couple of the pirates started work on building the lip/gum-synching apparatus, whilst the Captain lined up the rest of the crew beside the creature.

'Right, me beauties. I'll be needing a volunteer to slither down the whale's fishy throat. You know me – normally I'd be first to step forward, but it'll look pretty suspicious if I'm not there to hand him over, won't it? So – who's it going to be?'

The pirates did their usual trick of staring at the horizon and pretending not to hear.

'Sometimes I think I'd be better off crewing the ship with lobsters,' said the Pirate Captain, with a sorry shake of his head. 'Well then. We'll decide this like pirates. You in the green ... you can start.' He nodded at the pirate in green.

'I went to the shops and I bought a cutlass,' said the pirate in green.

'I went to the shops,' said the sassy pirate, 'and I bought a cutlass and some brass buckles.'

'I went to the shops,' said the albino pirate, 'and I bought a cutlass, some brass buckles and some transfers ...'

It wasn't the fastest way to reach a decision and in the past it had proved costly in battle situations, but the Pirate Captain was a stickler for pirate traditions. Technically it was the pirate with a squint who made the first mistake, but the Pirate Captain decided to send the pirate in red inside the whale, because he was sick of his surly backchat.

'Can I take a magazine to read?' said the pirate in red,

clambering into the whale's gaping maw.

'Sorry, lad. No light in there, is there? You'll ruin your eyes,' said the Pirate Captain cheerily. 'Mind your head on the epiglottis!' he added, giving the pirate in red an encouraging shove.

An eerie keening sound washed across the deck as the pirate in red headed for the gloom of the whale's innards.

'What in the blue blazes is that racket?' said the Pirate Captain.

'I think it's whale song!' said Jennifer.

'It's beautiful!' said the pirate in green, entranced.

'We can't just give him to Ahab to chop up! Not a noble creature like this, capable of such magnificent music!' said the pirate with a poetic bent.

'It's just *moaning*,' said the Pirate Captain, snorting and pulling an unimpressed face.

'Couldn't we get him to apologise to Ahab as well?' said Jennifer. 'He could say "Sorry about the leg, Ahab. Accidents happen. No hard feelings, eh?" and then Ahab might let him off.'

The Pirate Captain rolled his eyes, because if there was one thing guaranteed to make his crew go gooey, it was creatures. The pirates had once spent an entire adventure pestering the Captain to buy them a parrot, only for him to find it two weeks later being used as a fuse on one of the boat's cannons. But by this point in his piratical career he had learnt that there wasn't much point arguing with the lads once they had their hearts set on something.

'*Fine*. If it really makes you feel better,' said the Pirate Captain, rubbing his temples wearily. 'Just so long as we convince Ahab he's the real deal. He can do the Gettysburg Address for all I care.'

Thirteen

CANNIBAL CORAL
CRAWLS TO KILL!

The Nantucket town clock struck a quarter to midnight as the last few bits of ground-up pirate bone ran through Cutlass Liz's egg-timer.

'Put your backs into it, boys!' said the Pirate Captain. 'You're doing a great job. Obviously I'd love to help you drag the whale onto the docks, but its oily hide could do lasting damage to my magnificent beard. And us pirates without my beard would be like the Tower of London without those big crows – we'd most likely just collapse in a heap.'

The crew let out a collective grunt and with a final heave pushed the whale over the side of the *Lovely Emma* and onto the dock's slippery cobblestones. Mindful that good pirating is all about the spectacle, the Pirate Captain had covered the creature with a big white sheet, so that he could unveil their prize with a flourish.

There was quite a crowd waiting for them. Ahab and his whalers were there, stony-faced as ever. Cutlass Liz was there, tapping her watch and looking cross. And there were a few assorted hangers-on who had just turned up to see what all the fuss was about.

'I hope you've got me here for a good reason,' said Ahab, looking moody in pyjamas and nightcap.

'Where's my money?' said Cutlass Liz, pointedly sharpening a big knife on a leather strap. 'And what have you got under that sheet?'

'The answer to all our problems!' said the Pirate Captain triumphantly, and with a theatrical jerk of his wrist he pulled the billowing sheet aside. There was a bit of a stunned silence.

'That's not six thousand doubloons,' said Cutlass Liz.

'It's a whale!' said the albino pirate helpfully.

'And not just any whale!' said the Pirate Captain, pointing at Ahab. 'But the brute who ate your leg off!'

Ahab looked the creature up and down. He circled round it a couple of times. He got out a little pair of half-moon spectacles and peered at it closely.

'I'm not convinced,' he muttered.

The Pirate Captain shrugged. 'I thought you might say that, but I can prove it.' He gave the sassy pirate a wink to get him ready with the lip-synching device. 'Because this whale will confess to the crime himself!'

'Pardon?' said Ahab.

'Isn't that so, whale? You've got something to say? Hmmm?' said the Pirate Captain, playing to the crowd a little as the sassy pirate started to work the ingenious system of pulleys and gears and bits of rope that made the whale's jaw jerk up and down.

'I have, Pirate Captain!' said the whale in what to the onlookers seemed a surprisingly reedy voice for such a huge beast.

'He's not as good at doing voices as me,' the Pirate Captain whispered to the scarf-wearing pirate. 'Though to be fair, it's difficult to sound genuinely oceanic.'

'First,' said the whale/pirate, 'I'd like to say how under-rated the pirate in red is. In my whale's opinion I would say he is the best pirate in the whole crew.'

The Pirate Captain scowled, because this wasn't exactly the way they'd rehearsed it.

'One of the reasons he's so good is that he bothers to learn the proper nautical terms for things, and can tell the difference between the galley and the steering wheel. Can you do that, Pirate Captain?'

'Aarrrr,' said the Pirate Captain defensively. 'Of course.'

'I mean to say, you wouldn't have any problem telling the mizzenmast from the foremast? And you'd never be heard referring to the hull as "that bit which stops all the water getting in"?'

The Pirate Captain started to finger his cutlass in what he hoped was a menacing fashion, but then he remembered that just because the pirate was inside the whale it didn't mean he could *see* what the whale could see, so using a subtle visual threat was probably useless.

'And another reason the pirate in red is so good is because he has an imperious nose. Not, you notice, a "stentorian" nose because stentorian is a tone of voice.'

'Well, whale, I'm sure we all agree with you about how fantastic the pirate in red is,' said the Pirate Captain, through gritted gold teeth. 'It would certainly be a shame if anything terrible happened to him. Like, oh I don't know, spending the rest of our next adventure getting keel-hauled.[30] Or fed to sea cucumbers. Now, I think you have a message for Mister Ahab, don't you?'

'All right, I was getting to it,' said the whale/pirate testily. 'Ahab – I just wanted to say how sorry I am about the business when I ate your leg. I'd got a bit bored that day of plankton or squid or whatever it is I usually eat. I hope there's no hard feelings.'

The sassy pirate surreptitiously used the lip-synching apparatus to make the whale do a winning and apologetic grin. There was an expectant hush.

'Well,' said Ahab, scratching his scar, 'I suppose this must be the beast. Though he seems to have shrunk since I saw him last.'

'That's seawater for you,' said the Pirate Captain, thinking fast. 'I once dropped my favourite blousy shirt

---

30 Keel-hauling was actually a practice used more by the Royal Navy than pirates, and it was an attempt to escape this kind of barbarity that probably drove many sailors into piracy in the first place.

into a rock pool, and by the time I fished the thing out it wouldn't have fitted a baby.'

Ahab still looked slightly unconvinced.

The Pirate Captain hurriedly looked at his pocket watch. 'So then. It appears that just for once we've finished with a bit of time to spare. All that's left is for you' – he grinned as hopefully as he could at Ahab – 'to give us our reward, so that I can pay you' – he grinned as sexily as he could at Cutlass Liz – 'and then I can spend the rest of the adventure just messing about with my belly.'

But before the Pirate Captain could even begin to play about with his belly button, the whole dock started to shake, and there was a sound like a thousand cannonballs being dropped into a bucket. A wall of water rose up from the sea and crashed across the docks. Out from the churning swell came the tip of something white, and it kept on coming until there, rearing up on its tail, was the biggest whale any of the pirates had ever seen. If the pirates had been alive a hundred and fifty years later and had happened to be drawing the diagrams in biology textbooks, they would have said the whale was as tall as three double-decker buses stacked on top of each other, or about a half of one St Paul's Cathedral. But they weren't, so they just thought that the whale was really very big indeed.

The monster roared, lunged and came crashing down right on top of the *Lovely Emma*. All the onlookers scattered about, and most of the pirates tried to hide behind barrels.

'Oh dear,' said the Pirate Captain.

'Goodness me,' said the pirate with a scarf.

The whale rose up again, and with another resounding thump belly-flopped onto the boat.

'This is a bit of bad luck, isn't it, Captain?' said the pirate with gout.

'I hate to say I told you so,' said the fake whale/pirate in red, 'but if you will go about the place killing albatrosses, you have to expect this kind of thing.'

Just for once the Pirate Captain found himself agreeing with the mutinous swab. It did seem like a spectacular piece of cosmic bad luck for the white whale to turn up out of the blue like this, apparently for no better reason than to make his life a misery. He stared sadly at the *Lovely Emma*. Then he stared at the whale. A huge excited whale eye winked back at him. The Pirate Captain stared at the *Lovely Emma* again. And suddenly everything clicked into place in his piratical brain.

Fig. 1:
A lady whale

Fig. 2:
The Lovely Emma

Figure 1
Gigantic tail
Colossal flipper
Flirtatious mouth
Spray from the blowhole
The gentle echo of whale song

Figure 2
The banner from the Las Vegas show
The Captain's duvet put out to air
Dead eel wrapped around the bow
Burst waterpipe
A moaning leper

'The beast thinks our boat is a lady whale!' he cried.

There was a terrible creaking noise, and the *Lovely Emma* lurched this way and that.

'I don't think the boat is enjoying it all that much,' said the pirate with a scarf.

'But why would the man whale want to squash a lady whale like that?' asked the albino pirate. The Pirate Captain didn't think now was the moment to explain, because a horrifying thought suddenly flashed into his magnificent head: the Prize Ham was still nailed to the *Lovely Emma*'s mast.

'My ham! My beautiful ham!' roared the Pirate Captain. And before he had really thought things through, he found himself charging towards the *Lovely Emma* in a panic.

'What on earth is the fellow doing?' said Ahab, as the Captain streaked towards the boat.

'He's decided to show that whale who's boss!' exclaimed Jennifer. 'Yay! Go Pirate Captain!'

'Shouldn't you be doing that too, Mister Ahab?' said the pirate with long legs. 'Because of all of the cold-revenge-soothing-the-soul business?'

Ahab looked at the terrible gaping maw of the whale, and at its appalling chomping teeth. 'For some reason,' he said, 'upon seeing the beast, I do not find myself so inclined.'

'Is your Captain always like this?' asked Cutlass Liz, shaking her head in disbelief.

'Oh yes,' said the pirate in green confidently. 'He's very brave. He once took on the entire Royal Navy single-handed, whilst we were all asleep. They boarded us in the dead of night and stole our last few bottles of grog, and then the Pirate Captain fought them off but he was too late to save the grog. We didn't even know a thing about it until the next morning when we realised the grog was gone and he explained what had happened to us over breakfast. The whole fight had given him a terrible headache.'

About fifteen feet from the jetty, the Pirate Captain began to appreciate just how massive the white whale was. He himself was rightly famed across the Seven Seas for being able to fit an entire pork chop in his mouth, but the beast in whose shadow all the pirates now cowered looked as if it could fit an entire field of cows in its mouth all in one go, and maybe still have room to spare. Wondering just how wise it would be to interrupt something so gigantic right in the middle of it getting busy[31] – even for a cause as noble as saving his ham – the Pirate Captain reconsidered and did his best to try skidding to a halt, but the cobblestones were even more slippery now, and instead of stopping, the Captain simply went sliding right off the side of the dock and into the cold sea with a plaintive 'plop'.

---

[31] Different types of whales adopt different reproductive strategies. Male humpback whales sometimes blow a thick curtain of bubbles to try and block their intended mate from the view of other competing males. Whilst uninterested females have been observed to hide under boats and wait there until the males have all gone away. Smart creatures, male whales have never been observed trying to impress lady whales by writing books about pirates.

'Oh no,' said the pirate with a scarf, looking on distraught. 'I can't bear to look.'

The monstrous whale went on bouncing up and down on the boat. The onlookers gazed apprehensively at the churning sea, but there was no sign of the Captain.

'Arrrr,' muttered Ahab broodingly into the middle distance. 'That was a brave way to go. The good Captain must have known his was a path that could end only with the hangman's noose, or the murky depths of the ocean. Yet he paid it no mind! To risk everything in the pursuit of liberty and pleasure without constraint. Isn't that the very reason why he chose the life of a pirate?'

'Not really,' said the albino pirate, fighting back the tears. 'I think it was more just something to do.'

The water in the harbour was very dark. Not for the first time it occurred to the Pirate Captain that, given his line of work, he really should have learnt to swim by now. At one point he had actually spent entire adventures wearing armbands just in case this kind of situation cropped up, but somehow it never really struck the right bloodthirsty note. He flapped his arms uselessly for a while and then started to sink like a brick. A piece of seaweed got tangled up in his beard, and a little shoal of fish bobbed past his face. He was trying to decide if he would prefer '*A man like no other*' or '*He was a true original*' as the inscription on his gravestone, when he felt himself rush up through the water, break the surface, and fly through the air in a burst of spray. The white whale had waggled its great tail and flipped the Pirate Captain as if he were nothing more than a soggy pinball. He described a perfect piratical arc before coming thumping down onto the deck of the *Lovely Emma*. The Captain sat there for a moment, shook the kelp from his beard and looked about him in a daze.

'He's back!' cheered the pirate in green.

'And he's not even hurrying,' said the pirate with a hook for a hand. 'I'd like to see Black Bellamy stay that nonchalant when his boat was being attacked by the biggest whale in the world.'

As the Pirate Captain's vision cleared, he saw that he had landed right next to the mast where his Prize Ham was still nailed. He staggered to his feet, pulled out the nail, grabbed the ham in both arms and gave it a big hug. 'I'll never leave you alone again,' he promised in a hoarse whisper. The whale chose this touching moment to do a particularly energetic belly-flop onto the *Lovely Emma*'s aft, which sent her lurching sharply. The Pirate Captain hooked one arm around the mast and wondered what to do. He considered punching the whale on the nose, because he recalled something about that being their weak spot. But then he remembered how that might be sharks rather than whales. And also that it was probably apocryphal anyway. And of course whales don't really have noses.

The whale went on writhing about, half on the ship and half off. Its great twisted mouth was clashing and biting alarmingly close to the Pirate Captain now, and he swore he caught a glimpse of the remains of Ahab's leg trapped in one of the sharp molars. The creature snapped its jaws shut barely inches from where he was standing, and the Pirate Captain let out a terrified shriek and leapt into the air. He landed with a squelch on the whale's eyelid and clung on for dear life.

'Did you hear that high-pitched roar of defiance as he jumped onto its face?' said Jennifer.

'That,' said Ahab, 'is the most courageous man I ever saw.'

With a loud and slightly obscene groan, the beast started to slide back into the water. The Pirate Captain realised that his only chance now was to try and scale the fish's face and leap across the dock. He scrambled desperately against its rubbery flesh, hauling himself up inch by inch, but just as he was scrabbling for a hand-hold on the whale's furrowed brow, his shiny pirate boot skated across its skin and let out a horrendous squeak. It was a lot like when someone does that trick of scraping their nails down a blackboard. The Pirate Captain's sensitive teeth were so set on edge by this that he clamped his hands to his ears, and in the process dropped his Prize Ham. It bounced away down the whale's back.

'Hell's bells!' exclaimed the Pirate Captain, sprinting

along the top of the whale in pursuit. For one moment he thought he had it, but the ham flipped through the air and, with a sudden *sucking* sound, bounced straight into the whale's blowhole. The Captain knelt down and desperately tried to wiggle it free, but the thing was stuck fast.

'Come on, Pirate Captain!' cheered the watching pirates. 'This is no time for a snack. Give that whale a smack!'

As the Pirate Captain strained at the ham, the whale began to spasm and buck about in the water. Its tail thrashed wildly up and down. Its flippers windmilled in the air uselessly. Then an ear-splitting moan erupted from its mouth and the whale rolled from the sinking boat onto the dock, shuddering one last terrible death spasm before lying still on the cobbles.

The Pirate Captain slid down its cheek and landed in front of the crowd of pirates and onlookers. They all started clapping, so he did a little bow.

'That was brilliant!' said the pirate with a scarf.

'You've killed the white whale!' exclaimed Ahab.

'How did you know what to do, Captain?' said the albino pirate.

'Aaarrrr,' said the Captain, emptying some seawater from his hat. 'Well. As I may have pointed out before, I'm not a *complete* idiot, you know.'

The crowd all looked at him expectantly. The Pirate Captain thought for a bit and then put on an authoritative tone of voice. 'Any seafaring type knows that the blowhole of the whale is essential for expelling whale wee. It was clear to me that if I could block the blowhole, the whale's bladder would swell up and explode.'

'And the way you made it look like you were really quite hapless whilst you were doing it,' said Cutlass Liz, with a playful slap of his shoulder, 'so that the whale wouldn't cotton on to your clever plan. Genius, Captain.'

'*That* was the beast who ate my leg,' said Ahab, pointing to the dead whale.

'Arrrr. This probably looks bad,' said the Captain apologetically, 'but I can explain.'

Ahab wasn't listening. 'I am afraid, Pirate Captain, that you have been had. This creature,' and he pointed at the pirates' fake whale, 'has been masquerading as the real villain, even though he is innocent of the crime.'

Ahab turned to the pirate/whale.

'I can only guess at what motivations led you to try and take the blame for that brute's actions, but it was a noble thing to do. Misguided though you were, I think that shows real strength of character. It may be that I have misjudged you whales after all.' And for the first time that any of the pirates had witnessed, Ahab cracked a smile. He patted the whale on the side of its gigantic face.

'In fact,' he continued, 'I'd like it very much if you'd be a guest at my home. I'm a famous curmudgeon, but underneath it all I'm really quite lonely, and it would be nice to have some company about the place.'

'Um. All right then,' said the pirate/whale.

Everybody cheered this happy outcome, and

something of a carnival atmosphere broke out amongst the pirates. Ahab turned back to the Pirate Captain. He handed him a bulging bag of doubloons. 'Your reward, sir. You've earned it.'

The Pirate Captain looked at the doubloons wistfully for a moment, and then threw them over to Cutlass Liz. He watched the last bit of the *Lovely Emma* sink beneath the waves and heaved a forlorn sigh.

'Don't look so upset, Pirate Captain!' said Cutlass Liz, putting a consoling arm around his shoulder. 'You can always buy a new boat.'

The Pirate Captain shook his head. 'I haven't got so much as two pieces of eight to rub together.'

'You must have something?' said Cutlass Liz encouragingly.

'The ultimate treasure?'

'Is that one of those richer-in-spirit things about wet butterflies?'

'Something along those lines.'

'Not really my thing, I'm afraid. Come on, what's in those voluminous pockets of yours?'

The Pirate Captain emptied his pockets onto the top of a barrel. 'I've got a chocolate groat with fluff on it, a 'one child gets in free' voucher to see the lunatics at Bedlam, some seaweed, and an apple core. What kind of a boat can I get with that?'

'I think I've got just the thing,' said Cutlass Liz with a grin.

Fourteen

SHE LAUGHED HER WAY TO MURDER!

Later that night, back in the familiar if ramshackle surroundings of their old pirate boat, the pirates were all lying on deck looking at the stars.

'That constellation looks just like a tiny-headed horse who's swallowed a huge rectangle,' said the pirate in green.

'Rubbish. It looks like a beautiful mermaid lady,' said the sassy pirate.

'Oh, you think everything looks like a beautiful mermaid lady,' said the pirate with a scarf. The Pirate Captain stepped onto the deck wearing his dressing-gown and smoking a post-adventure cigar.

'Up late, lads,' he said, blowing a relaxed smoke ring. 'Don't forget – even us pirates need our beauty sleep.'

'Sorry, Captain. We were just discussing what that constellation looks like.' The pirate in green pointed at where they were looking. The Pirate Captain craned his neck and looked up.

'It looks just like my Prize Ham,' he said, a little sadly. The pirates all nodded in agreement.

'Sometimes I think there's nothing a good piece of ham can't do,' said the pirate with a scarf. 'The way that she bounced straight into the whale's blowhole. It was almost as if she were deliberately trying to sacrifice herself for you.'

'You mean like Baby Jesus?' asked the albino pirate, wide-eyed.

'I suppose so,' said the pirate with a scarf thoughtfully.

'Except Baby Jesus never had a delicious honey-roast glaze, did he? So in many ways my ham was a lot better than Baby Jesus ever was,' pointed out the Pirate Captain. He took off his pirate hat and lay down next to his crew.

'It's good to have the old boat back,' he said. 'I don't know why I ever let you lot talk me into getting a different one.'

'I'm glad there were too many barnacles on her for Cutlass Liz to chop her into firewood.'

'Good old barnacles.'

'I miss the *Lovely Emma*'s swimming pool though,' said the sassy pirate.

'And her panoramic views,' added the pirate in green.

'But I think we learnt a lot on this adventure, Pirate Captain,' said the scarf-wearing pirate, 'so it hasn't been a dead loss.'

'You're right,' said the Pirate Captain, closing his eyes and listening to the quiet rumble of the ocean. 'We learnt that getting into debt is not a matter to be taken lightly.'

'Also, we learnt that making an extravagant gesture to impress a girl is pretty stupid,' said the albino pirate.

'We tend to "learn" that on most adventures,' said the pirate with rickets.

'And most importantly of all we learnt the grass might look greener in showbusiness or whaling or something like that. But that when it comes down to it, you're often better off sticking with what you know,' said the pirate with a scarf.

'So long as what you know is kicking about the High Seas being a pirate, that is.'

'Oh yes, the lesson wouldn't apply if you had a regular job. In fact, anybody that did would be strongly advised to give it up right now and become a pirate themselves.'

With that the pirates went downstairs to do some shantying. And they were soon enjoying themselves so much that they barely even noticed when the pirate boat's mast fell down again.

*   *   *   *   *

Learn More About ...

Debt

Like the Pirate Captain, more people than ever are getting into serious debt, with the accompanying risks of depression, worry and not being able to buy things that you want.

- If you're desperate about debt, call the National Debtline free on 0808 808 4000.
- The snappily-titled Consumer Credit Counselling Service (www.cccs.co.uk) will help turn that debt frown upside-down by talking about budgeting and that.

Remember – no matter how bad things seem, there's always a way out. Just look at the Pirate Captain – a whale attacked his boat and he was fine in the end!

Whale Conservation

The pirates' adventure was set in the olden days, when it was all right to go whaling. But nowadays things are different – there are thought to be around 570,000 sperm whales left in the sea, down from 2,000,000 in the 1940s. If you're concerned about whales (sperm or otherwise), you can help make a difference:

- Join the Whale and Dolphin Conservation Society

(www.wdcs.org). You'll get a whale-tail sticker!

- If you see a stranded whale, call the British Divers Marine Life Rescue on 01825 765 546. If they're not in, try the RSPCA (08705 555 999) or Environment Agency (0800 807 060). *Don't* throw stuff at the stranded whale.

- Try to restrict your consumption of whale meat and ambergris to special occasions.

Nantucket

The pirates didn't get much of a chance to explore the historic town of Nantucket, but there's nothing to stop *you* from finding out more!

- The Nantucket Island Chamber of Commerce have loads of information about visiting the island, along with a low-resolution map and live weather updates. They also publish the official 288-page guidebook.

- The mission of the Nantucket Historical Association (www.nha.org) is to preserve the island's unique history and tell people about it. Pop to their website and have fun finding out more.

- Nantucket is also famous for its cranberry bogs. Why not pour yourself a cool glass of cranberry juice and sip it while thinking about harpoons?

Acknowledgements

Thanks to:

Rob Adey, Chloe Brown, Cilla McIntosh, Rodney Brown, Sam Brown, Matt Evans, Helen Garnons-Williams, Fiona Hankey, Yvonne Kee, David Murkin, Rebecca Murkin, Claire Paterson and Brigid Way.

Don't forget to check out these other great titles in 'The Pirates!' series, all available direct from W&N and Random House (US) or at your local book store:

The Pirates! In An Adventure With Scientists
The Pirates! In An Adventure With Rasputin
The Pirates! In An Adventure With Americans
The Pirates! In An Adventure With Ice Cream
The Pirates! In An Adventure With Railroads
The Pirates! In An Adventure With the Green Ghost
The Pirates! In An Adventure With the Village of Fear
The Pirates! In An Adventure In Tir Na Nog
The Pirates! In An Adventure With Pigs
The Pirates! In An Adventure With Golems
The Pirates! In An Adventure With Rabbis
The Pirates! In An Adventure With Rabbits
The Pirates! In An Adventure With Mondays
The Seven Habits Of Highly Effective Pirates
The Pirates! In An Adventure With Eskimos
The Pirates! In An Adventure With Cannibals
Watch Yourself, Pirate Captain!
The Pirates Get Sexy
The Pirates! In An Adventure With Space Pirates
Back To Pirate Academy, Pirate Captain!
Back To Pirate Academy 2, Pirate Captain!
Back To Pirate Academy 3, Pirate Captain!

Back To Pirate Academy 4, Pirate Captain!
Back To Pirate Academy 5, Pirate Captain!
Back To Pirate Academy 6, Pirate Captain!
Back To Pirate Academy 7, Pirate Captain!
The Pirates! In An Adventure With Murder
The Pirates! On Holiday
The Pirates! In An Adventure With the Stock Market
Pirate Captain and Son
The Pirates! In An Adventure With Lingerie
The Pirates Ride Out
The Pirates Go Ape
The Pirates! In An Adventure With Your Mother
The Pirates! In An Adventure With Freemasons
The Pirates! In An Adventure With Puppets
The Pirates! In An Adventure With Automatons
The Pirates! In An Adventure With Prussians
The Pirates! In An Adventure With Heavy Petting
I, Pirate Captain
The Pirates Go Fruit Picking
The Pirates! In An Adventure With A Very Windy Day
The Pirates! In An Adventure With Football
The Pirates and the Blacksmith's Daughter
The Pirates! In An Adventure With Gypsies
Ring A Ring Of Pirates
Half A Pound Of Tupenny Rice, Half A Pound Of Pirates
The Pirates! In An Adventure With The Thieves Of Time
The Pirates! In An Adventure With Haute Couture
The Pirates! In Two Hours 'Til Doomsday
Pirates Down the Rhine
The Pirates Make A Midnight Escape
The Ballad Of the Pirate Captain
The Pirates! In An Adventure With A Secret
A Stitch In Time Saves Pirates
The Pirates Have Egyptian Capers
The Pirates! In An Adventure With the Triads
The Pirates! In An Adventure With the Pope
The Pirates! In An Adventure With Spring-Heel Jack
The Pirates' Underwater Adventure
The Pirates and the Citadel Of Chaos
The Pirates! In An Adventure With the G.O.P.
The Pirates! In An Adventure With Tunnels
The Pirates Holiday Special
The Pirate Treasury

The Pirates! In An Adventure With A Mysterious Gas
The Pirates! In An Adventure With Spectral Hands
The Pirates! In An Adventure With Mongol Hordes
The Pirates! In An Adventure With Spiders
Think Fast, Pirate Captain!
Black Bellamy Rides Again
Pirate vs. Pirate
The Pirates! In Mayhem Cove
The Pirates! In An Adventure With A Steep Hill
The Pirates Play Dead
The Pirates! In An Adventure With Nuts
The Pirates! In An Adventure With Wasps
You Can Do It, Pirate Captain!
The Pirates' Super T-shirts
The Pirates Sleep With the Lights On
The Pirates On Halloween
The Pirates Making It
The Pirates! In An Adventure With the Political Supremacy Of the
    Bourgeoisie
The Pirates! In An Adventure With Risk Management
The Pirates! Commit A Series Of Horrific Atrocities
The Pirates! In An Adventure With Geordies
Pirate Fever!
The Pirates and the Edge Of Reason
The Pirates! In An Adventure With Public Sanitation
The Pirates! In An Adventure With Chess
The Pirates Strut Their Stuff
The Pirates! In An Adventure With An Ant
The Pirates! In An Adventure With A Harlequin
The Pirates! In An Adventure With A Damp Smell
The Pirates: Going Straight
The Pirates Embrace Diversity
P.I.R.A.T.E.
The Pirates Justify Themselves
The Pirates! In An Adventure With Gigolos
The Pirates! In An Adventure With Femmes Fatales
Jet Set Pirates!
The Moon's A Doubloon
The Pirates! In A Worker's Utopia
The Pirates! In An Adventure With Eugenics
Quite So, Pirate Captain
The Pirates! In An Adventure With the Alamo
The Pirates! In An Adventure With Rita, Sue & Bob Too

The Pirates! In An Adventure Down Mexico Way
The Pirates! In An Adventure With the Special Olympics
The Pirates! In An Adventure With Catastrophe Theory
The Pirates! In An Adventure With Slum Landlords
Konichiwa, Pirate Captain!
The Pirates! In An Adventure With Difference Engines
Bladderwrack!
The Cutlass and the Rose
The Pirates' Rainy Day Indoors
The Pirates! In An Adventure With Spies
Stone The Crows, Pirate Captain!
The Pirates Are Killing Music
Black Bellamy's Gambit
The Pirates! In An Adventure With Smugglers
The Pirates! Learn German In Five Easy Lessons
The Pirates! Shoot Horses With Cannons
This Little Pirate Went To Market
The Pirates! Run Amok
The Pirates! In An Adventure With the Jungle Of Destiny
The Pirates! Fanny About On A Yacht
The Pirates! Remember the Olden Days
The Pirates! In An Adventure With the Jorvik Centre
The Pirates! In An Adventure With the Spelling Bee
The Pirates! In An Adventure With Disguises & Make-up
The Pirates! In An Adventure With Ponies & Riding
The Pirates! In An Adventure With Bikes
The Pirates! In An Adventure With Jennifer Garner
The Pirates! In An Adventure With The Goonies
The Pirates! In An Adventure With Foot & Mouth
The Pirates! In An Adventure With the Lubbock Lake Landmark
The Pirates! In An Adventure With Maths & Numbers
The Pirates! In An Adventure With Lola Montez
The Pirates! In An Adventure With the Kretzmer Syndrome
The Pirates! In An Adventure With the Honey Trap
The Pirates! In An Adventure With the Girls From Café Noir
The Pirates! In An Adventure With Skeletons
The Pirates! In An Adventure With Shaft
The Pirates Do Dallas
The Pirates! In An Adventure With Lazy Post-modernism
The Pirates! In An Adventure With Monkey's Delight
The Pirates! In An Adventure With A Spooky Eye
The Pirates! In An Adventure With Brockwell Infants School
The Pirates! In An Adventure That Goes Wrong

The Pirates! In An Adventure With the Circus Of Death
The Pirates! In An Adventure With the Path Of Least Resistance
The Pirates! In An Adventure With the Empire State Human
The Pirates! In An Adventure With the Dignity Of Labour (Parts 1–4)
The Pirates Colouring-in Book
The Pirates! In An Adventure With the Culture Of Fear
The Pirates! Build A Base In the Woods
The Pirates! In An Adventure With Unshaven Men
The Pirates! Have Been Running With Scissors Again
The Pirates! In An Adventure With the Red Hand Gang
The Pirates! In An Adventure With the IRS
The Pirates! In An Adventure With that Man On Beta
The Pirates! In An Adventure With the Bronze Girls Of the Shaolin
The Pirates! In A Big Top Adventure
The Pirates! In An Adventure With Jazzy Jeff
The Pirates! In An Adventure With Boggle
The Pirates! In An Adventure With Richard Dawkins
The Pirates! Together In Electric Dreams
You've Got To Fight For Your Right To Pirate
The Pirates! In An Adventure With the Cartesian Theatre
Leave It To Pirates
The Pirates! And The Mystery Of The Stuttering Parrot
The Pirates! And The Secret Of Phantom Lake
The Pirates! In An Adventure In Idaho
The Pirates! In An Adventure With Mormons
Oy Vey, Pirate Captain!
A Very Peculiar Pirate
The Pirates! Did Not Mean To Say That Out Loud
The Pirates! In An Adventure With Zombies
The Pirates! In An Adventure With Cowboys
The Pirates! In An Adventure With Richard Nixon
Don't Stop Now, Pirate Captain!
The Pirates and the Phenomenological Garden
The Pirates! In An Adventure Down The Anchor
The Pirates! Are Overdoing It A Bit

Join the **Captain's Cutlass Club** and receive a free **Pirate Badge**. This attractive three-colour badge, pinned to your blazer lapel or jumper, will excite the interest and comment of all your friends! Send a self-addressed envelope to **Orion House, 5 Upper Saint Martin's Lane, London, WC2H 9EA (UK)**.

The MIGRATORY COURSE
of the
ACCURSED
GREAT WHITE WHALE

THE ROCKIES

THE GREAT PLAINS

RIVER NILE

More Fierce

Howsawobbling Varmint

LAS VEGAS